The Shadow School

By Briar Campbell

All characters, settings, and events in this book were created as fictional. Any resemblance to real life people, places, or happenings are coincidental except for a few mentions of historic events, famous names, and the basic plot of the Ray Bradbury story
"A Sound of Thunder" (Copyright 1952, Renewed 1980 by Ray Bradbury).

Cover image by Junel Aceres

Haven Point High School Fallout Shelter

During the Cold War, the town of Haven Point had constructed an underground fallout shelter under its high school. If nuclear war were to strike, the school shelter would act as a designated living area for the best and brightest students in the area as they begin to rebuild civilization.

To get to its entrance under Haven Point High School, one must descend down three flights of stairs, where they will find a reinforced steel door in the school's landing space in the basement. Currently, the shelter door is locked tight, and knowledge of the landing space by the entrance has dwindled from memory of everyone except the occasional trespasser—like Sandy Meade.

Sandy Meade was reported missing in 1989, though the exact date of her disappearance is unknown. She was a lonely junior at Haven Point and a common target for bullying by more popular students. She had discovered a key for the shelter door, and she decided to explore the shelter on her own. It became her secret hideaway. As the bullying worsened, she spent more and more time exploring the maze of empty halls and classrooms. At some point during the year, she went down to her usual hiding place and never came out.

Some people say that Sandy was murdered or she committed suicide. Others believe that she still lives in those halls, prowling around below the school in the only place that she had kept herself safe from the torment of her classmates.

Chapter 1

"It's a horrible idea," Ruby said during lunch. "You have no idea what's down there."

"That's why we're going," Evan said, his positive mood not the least bit dampened by Ruby's hard-biting attitude.

"It's too dangerous," Ruby declared. "It'll be full of collapsed tunnels and toxic sewage. Maybe you'll get lucky and find a nest of rabid rats."

"You think a bomb shelter couldn't withstand rats?"

"It couldn't withstand anything. It's never been built."

"Listen, Ruby," Evan said, "you know that key I found? I tested it, and it fits. There's gotta be something behind that door. This is a once-in-a-lifetime opportunity." He motioned to Faye. "Tell her, Faye."

"Once in a lifetime," Faye echoed. She knew better than to argue with Evan about exploring under the school. Nothing she or Ruby could say would change his mind. Evan had set on this goal since long before Faye moved here, and nothing would convince him to abandon it.

"So, we need to figure out a plan," Evan said. "We'll need gear for navigating underground. Like lights. What kind of lights do cavers use?"

"You'll have to ask the cavers," Faye answered, resting her elbows on the table.

Ruby frowned. "You aren't actually planning to go with him?" she asked.

"Yeah, I am," Faye answered. "I want to see the shelter, too."

"God, if you two were in a horror movie, you'd be in deep trouble."

"So would you," Evan retorted, "because smug deniers get killed, too."

"Well, I'm not going down there, so my chances for getting killed from exploring sewage are zero."

"Understood." Evan pulled out his phone and started shopping for some professional caver gear.

Chapter 2

On Saturday morning, Coach Fitzroy opened the doors by the gym at five a.m. for football practice. Evan and Faye slid in several minutes after a couple of the jocks, then loitered by the vending machines until the coach and the players headed for the changing room. After that, they headed for the stairwell that would lead to the entrance.

Evan had hinted about another teammate, so they waited at the top of the stairs, munching on peanut butter sandwiches and gulping down protein smoothies. At that predawn hour, the toothpaste-green tiled walls looked like they were covered with soot. Faye wondered idly if they would look just as ghoulish underground without the rays of the sun to cast upon them. The shelter supposedly had sunlamps, but she imagined they would look gloomier in comparison.

"Did you make a will?" Evan asked.

"No."

"I did. I want to make sure that my money will go to my grandma and not my stepdad."

"Did you take it to a lawyer?" Faye asked. "They can't enforce it if you didn't make it official."

"If anything happens, you can make sure the money goes to Grandma. Or Ruby can," Evan decided. Both Faye and Ruby got along well with his grandmother.

"I don't care who gets my stuff," Faye replied, in answer to her post-death plans, or lack of them.

"Your parents will, I guess. Being absentee parents, they can't piss you off that much."

As Faye murmured no, the third adventurer arrived.

"Hey, Marcus," Faye greeted as she and Evan stood up. Marcus Roy—or Homeschool Marcus, as the kids in her class sometimes called him—had started classes at Norton University last year at age sixteen, then, according to rumor, dropped out because of anxiety problems.

"Hi." Marcus looked nervous at the moment. He fumbled with his heavy backpack, which was stuffed full of backup supplies. A neon-green fleece jacket popped up from the top of the pack, preventing the zipper from closing all the way. "I'm glad I brought these," he said, as if talking to himself.

Once they reached the bottom of the stairs, Marcus pulled out two more neon-green fleece jackets and thrust them at Faye and Evan. "You weren't really planning on going in there without brighter clothing, were you?"

Faye's T-shirt had little dabs of color on it. Evan, though, had dressed in clothes as black as a ninja's outfit. Faye laid her backpack on the floor and slipped on her new jacket

"We have lights," Evan justified.

"What kind of lights?" Marcus asked.

Evan got out his LED flashlight and showed it to him. "This'll last up to thirty hours," Evan recited.

"Same," Faye echoed as she readjusted her ponytail.

"That's at the lowest setting," Marcus reminded them. "You are aware we'll be underground in pitch darkness, right?"

"Yeah."

"Have either of you been in pitch darkness? I mean, with absolutely no light?"

"I have," Faye answered.

Evan turned, surprised by this answer. "Since when?"

"It's a long and uninteresting story," Faye said. To Marcus, she said, "You're going to have to leave some of your stuff here."

Marcus knelt by his backpack and started rummaging. He took out his phone, two more flashlights, three thermoses, three water bottles, five packed lunches, multiple trail mix packs, multiple cords, several first aid kits, a GPS guide, a lockpick, two pairs of rain boots, several hats, and several pairs of rubber gloves.

"We did remember to bring food and water," Evan said. "And our shoes are fine."

Marcus looked at their heavy combat boots and nodded. He put one of each item back into the bag, except for three of the packed lunches and all the trail mixes. Faye helped him shove the rest of his things behind a stack of chairs.

Evan, meanwhile, had turned to the door. He removed the key from his jeans pocket. There was little reason to marvel over the key's appearance; it was chunky but otherwise unadorned except for the yellow ribbon tied in the keyhole.

Evan inserted the chunky key in the center of the slot and turned the lever. The door opened soundlessly.

Entrance

Chapter 3

Evan took his flashlight, notched it to its highest setting, and shone the beam into the door. Circling the beam revealed a hallway with smooth concrete walls and a solid, dry floor. The hallway extended until it disappeared far beyond his sight.

He took his phone out and snapped a picture, which he promptly sent to Ruby with a text.

Toxic sewage. Hah!

Faye noticed that Marcus had averted his eyes, trying not to peer too far into the deep hallway. Evan must have regaled him with stories of Sandy Meade waiting to pounce on anyone who dared enter her shelter. Or someone had.

"Would you like to go first?" she asked Evan, though she knew fully well that Evan would.

He prepared himself for his first step, but before he could enter, Marcus pulled him back. "Someone's coming." Evan's face skewed to an expression of disbelief, but Marcus was pointing behind them.

The three teenagers heard the furtiveness behind the steps.

"Aw, hell," Evan murmured. He dashed to the bottom of the stairwell and shouted up, "Hey, this room is taken!"

Connor Barrows emerged into view first, which set Evan to bristling in irritation. Connor was the type of person Evan despised: no imagination and perfectly happy with it. Evan had no patience for people who bragged about how boring and well-adjusted they were.

"Piss off, Newport. You don't own this space," Connor protested. "We have just as much right to use it as you do."

"We got here first." The last thing Evan needed was Connor butting in on his adventure, proclaiming how ridiculous it was. "Find some other place to hang out."

"Right, because what you guys are doing is so important. Summoning the dead or some kind of role-playing crap." Connor craned his neck out to catch a glimpse of what exactly they were doing.

"It's a school project," Evan said through clenched teeth. Technically true, as it took place on school grounds, and rediscovering history surely counted as a project. surely counted as a project.

"Ew. Are you guys spying on us?" That high-pitched, bubbly voice came from Leann Rivers. The pretty, fresh-faced girl lit into view. She stared at them with that amazement while carefully keeping her distance from the odder-looking classmates.

"You know what I think?" Connor said. "I think there's something down there you don't want us to see."

"He had to choose today to think," Evan said.

"I heard that." Connor reached the bottom of the stairs. Evan and Faye automatically blocked him, but Connor pushed through them. "Wuh-hoah."

He took in the sight of the open vault door and the cavernous hallway, with Marcus standing frozen at the entrance. He turned to look at Leann, then lowered his gaze to Faye.

"You're going into the bomb shelter," Connor stated.

Leann stepped down the final few stairs and joined Connor at his side. "Ohmygod."

"Yeah." Connor sounded impressed. Faye had not expected that. Usually, the meathead types at their school never acknowledged that anything existed outside their meathead interests in sports and popularity with girls.

"It looks dark in there," Leann observed.

"It is dark in there," Marcus said. "That's why . . ." He left his statement unfinished when he spotted Evan shaking his head, warning him not to volunteer information.

Evan cut in with a rude ahem. "I believe this takes priority over your plans. So, it's time for you to go."

"And what if I don't?"

"Why would you want to stay? Aren't you too grown-up to join in our role-playing game?"

"Doesn't matter," Connor said. "I know something about you that you don't want other people finding out. That means that you can't make me do anything."

Marcus sucked in a noisy breath.

"By the time you get to anyone, it'll be your word against ours," Faye pointed out. "Coach Fitzroy has the team running laps on Elder Street and Saturday School is meeting in the library. That's on the other side of the building," she hastily added because she was sure Connor did not know where the library was.

"But I bet Newport has pictures," Connor said as he snatched Evan's phone. Faye reached forward to block him. The phone flipped out of their grasp and landed—screen-face down—onto the concrete floor.

"Thanks a lot," Evan said. He lifted up the phone, which revealed a heavy crack slicing through the blackened screen.

"Guys!"

The other three turned to Marcus. "Where's Leann?" Connor asked, finally noticing his girlfriend's disappearance.

"She went in there," Marcus said, pointing to the endless hallway behind the vault door.

"Are you kidding?" Faye asked.

"I called her name, but she didn't answer," Marcus said.

"You're lying. This is a trick, right?" Connor demanded to know.

"Don't think so," Evan mumbled, still in his mourning pose over his phone. "Marcus is a crappy liar."

"She couldn't have gotten far," Faye said. "Not without a flashlight."

"Her phone . . ." Connor said, his voice cracking.

Faye refused to repeat the conversation about the absolute pitch darkness. "Call her."

He picked up his own phone.

A distant, peppy song started up, the sound coming deep from in the dark corridor.

"Leann!" Connor dashed in. Faye, Evan, and Marcus quickly gathered their tools and followed him in.

Faye clicked on her light first and soon found Connor. The peppy song grew louder as they journeyed farther down the hallway. Faye barely managed to avoid colliding into Connor when he stopped. She positioned the light down to the source of the music.

Connor crouched down and nudged Leann's abandoned phone into his hands.

She ran in here. And she has no light. These thoughts baffled Faye. She could have sworn that Leann was just as nervous about the darkness as Marcus. Did she really think she could find her way around without any light, without any way to contact anyone, without any hint of what she would find or where she would go?

"That's not good," Evan said as his flashlight beam joined hers.

Connor acted first. He shoved the phone in his jacket pocket and sprinted forward.

"Wait!" Faye ran after him again because otherwise he, too, would have gotten lost. Evan and Marcus trailed after them, unveiling their own flashlights.

They saw the wall before Connor did. Connor barely avoided slamming into it.

He stopped, breathless.

Marcus retrieved his extra flashlight from his backpack and handed it to Connor. Connor stared at it dumbly for a couple of seconds before he took it.

"Look," Evan whispered to Faye, aiming the flashlight back the way they had come. The vault entrance had disappeared from view, giving the impression that the four of them had gotten stranded in this corner.

"Someone should be keeping track of this," Marcus said. Automatically assuming that 'someone' referred to himself, he pulled up a drawing app. He traced a straight line down a grid.

There was nowhere to turn except right. Evan took the lead while Faye drifted to the back of the group, mainly to make sure Marcus did not get so caught up in his mapmaking that he would be left behind.

This segment of the hallway opened after about ten paces, branching out in three directions. Evan stepped into the wider crossing. He moved the flashlight beam along the walls and revealed lockers lining the hallways up ahead, interspersed with doors that held numbers **10** and **8** down the left wall and **9** and **7** at the right.

"Ladies and gentlemen," he gleefully announced, "I present the bomb shelter."

Entrance

Chapter 4

"Hey, Leann?" Connor called. His voice ricocheted through the empty halls. "Leann?"

He charged farther down the main hall. When he turned back, he realized the others continued to follow him. "Why don't you search the other halls?"

"We're not splitting up," Evan said. "That's horror movie lesson 101."

"Whatever, mouth breather," Connor scoffed.

If that's some attempt to let him go on his own, he might succeed before the morning's over, Faye thought. Common decency prevailed for now, though. They stuck with him.

Evan explored the walls as they passed by another classroom. Soon, his light hit a slightly wider door, labeled **Ladies**.

"I bet she's in there," Connor said. His spirits lifted at this rational conclusion. Leann could not have traveled any farther than this. She must be in the bathroom, waiting for the others to find her.

He looked over at Faye. "Are you going in or not?"

Faye made a displeased grunt, but she pushed through the door. "Leann? Are you in here?" She heard no sound that indicated the bathroom was occupied, but she walked farther in, letting the door swing shut.

Out of habit, she fumbled to the side for a light and flipped the tabbed switch. Only when the lights blazed on did she stop to consider how weird it was to see the room so brightly lit.

"Did you just turn on a light?" Evan asked through the door.

"Yeah."

"Is anyone in there?"

"No."

Evan came in, stumbling to a stop when he cast his squinted look over the room, which bore three stalls, two sinks, and a mirror.

He flinched as he heard a sudden splash of water, only to notice from the corner of his eye that Faye had tested the taps at one of the sinks. The water streamed out clear and unimpeded. Then she picked up one of the plain, brown boxes and opened it, sniffing at the square bar of soap.

"Hey, guys," Evan called. "You should see this!"

"Why?" Connor asked, bored. "Is Leann in there or not?"

"Not, but you should see this room."

He heard Connor grumble. Meanwhile, Faye checked the toilet stalls. A plenitude of toilet paper rolls stacked against the wall. She unwrapped one roll from its plain-brown wrap, tore off a square, and dropped it into the toilet. She pressed the flusher and watched the square disappear down the hole.

Marcus had heard the flush and asked with incredulous awe, "Is the plumbing still working?"

"Flawlessly," Evan assured him. "Unlike upstairs. We're like second-class citizens in our own school."

This allowed Marcus to overcome his concern about privacy in the women's bathroom and peek in.

"Look at this," Evan said. "Everything here is squeaky clean. No dirt, no scum, no rust."

"You think the janitors clean here?" Marcus suggested.

Evan crossed over to look inside the men's room. He reported it was in the same pristine condition as the ladies' room.

"So what if it's clean?" Connor asked.

"Someone else has been down here," Marcus explained.

"Yeah, Leann."

"Leann must be on a furious cleaning streak," Evan said.

"What did you say?" Connor asked.

"Never mind. Let's move on."

Chapter 5

They traveled farther down the main hallway. Marcus wanted to check the classrooms, but Connor declared it to be a waste of time.

They continued on the main hall until it came to an abrupt end. A bronze plaque covered the wall in front of them. It showed an etched outline of the United States, with Alaska and Hawaii bunched beside it on the left corner, and the words underneath eulogizing "Semper Fidelis."

"Where should we go?" Evan asked tiredly.

Marcus held up the map to give the others a closer look at what he had already drawn.

"The pattern seems to follow a similar layout to the school. If we round the hallway to the right, it'll lead us back to the entrance. I'm not sure about going left."

"So, we were going the wrong way just now?" Connor wanted to know.

"Shut up, Connor," Faye said. She hoisted her backpack and marched to the arm of the hallway extending to the right.

As she traveled on, Faye saw more lockers and more classroom doors. Marcus followed closely behind her while Evan herded Connor along with them. They reached another corner and turned.

She encountered a break in the wall but stopped when she realized it was not just another doorway.

It was a staircase. Leading down.

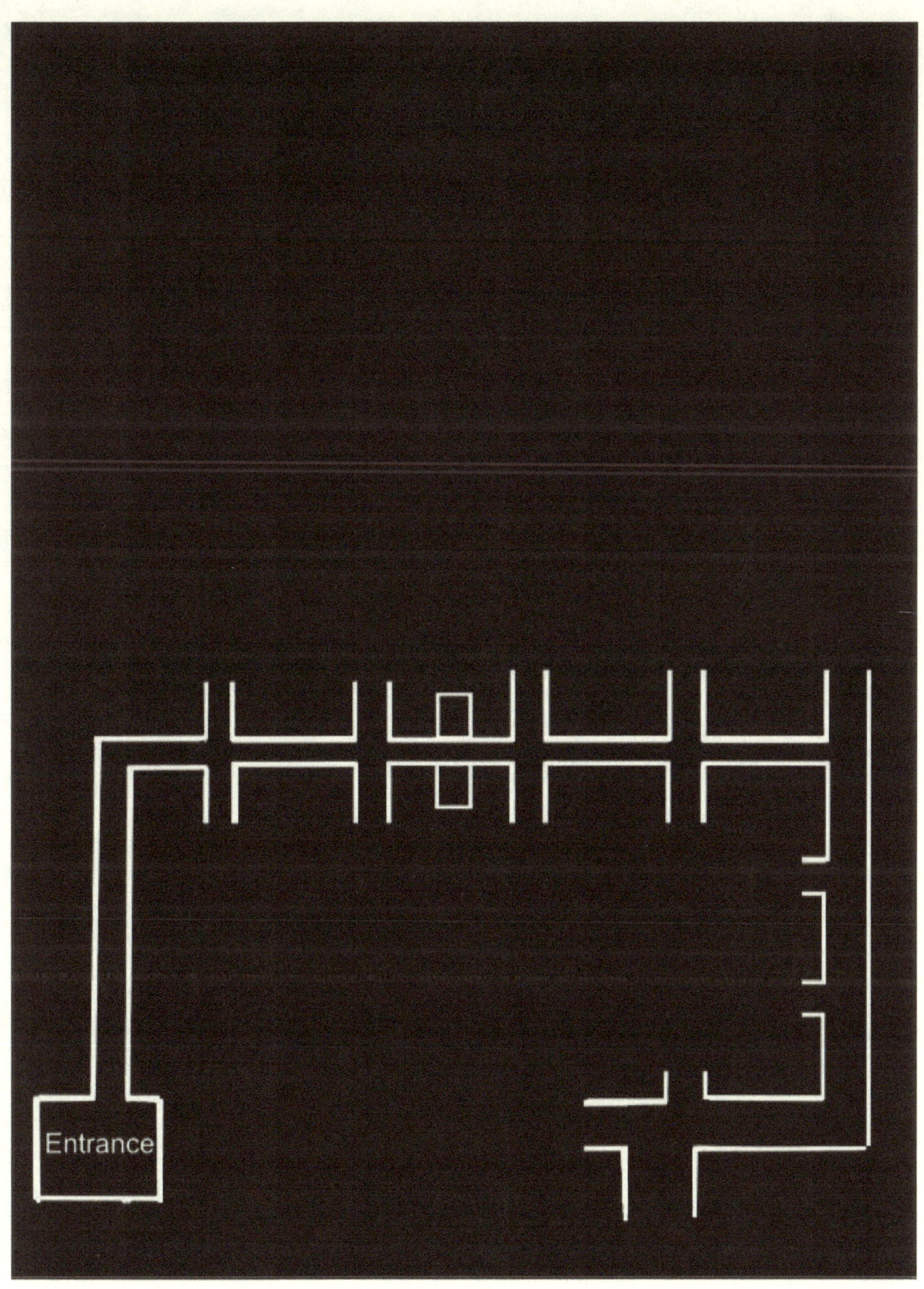
Entrance

Chapter 6

Evan spoke first. "I don't think we'll be able to cover the entire shelter in one day." They had all come to that realization, but only Evan spoke it.

"Would she go down there?" Faye felt ridiculous for asking. Connor would not know. He had not known Leann would ever go into the shelter in the first place.

"For all we know, she left the shelter already and went off to get her nails done while we're killing ourselves searching for her," Evan scoffed.

"That's not true," Connor rose to defend his girlfriend, but there was a note of doubt in his voice.

Evan caught on to that slight sign of doubt. "Had any arguments lately?"

"No."

"It's an important question. Is there any reason why Leann might not want you to find her?"

"No."

"We should stay on this floor for now," Marcus suggested. "It's simpler."

"We should do the exact opposite of what we think Leann would do," Evan reasoned.

"How do we do that?" asked Connor, exasperated.

"Evan, you're overthinking this," Faye said.

"Oh, fine. Let's do what's easier!"

A metallic echo sounded below the stairs. It suggested to Faye that some horror villain was scraping his knife against the railing. She did not actually think that was the source of the sound—not seriously—but she could not yank herself away from that imagined scene.

"We should explore the rest of the hallway first," she decided. From the expressions on the guys' faces, it seemed they would accept it. Even Evan looked far less than eager to go down there.

Marcus added an opening to mark the stairway on his map.

Chapter 7

Evan opened the first door he came across. The lights immediately flickered on, exhibiting a huge open space with rows of troughs filled with dirt. Counters rimmed the walls, encumbered by more pits of dirt and gardening tools.

It did not appear that any seeds had been planted. All the seed packages the teens could spot were unopened. Evan picked up a packet of sunflower seeds for future snacking.

Faye checked the doors at the end of the room. One opened to a supply closet containing large bags of soil and longer utensils like rakes. Leaving that space for Marcus to explore, she went to the second door, which emitted a muted hum. She parted open the door, which made the hum more identifiable to the others in the garden room.

"Bees," she said matter-of-factly.

That caught Connor's attention. "Bees?"

Evan, of course, had to see it for himself. He peeked in and was confronted by a glass wall covered with a mass of bees swarming over each other under amber light.

"Would you shut the door?" Connor asked, more impatient than ever.

"They're behind a wall," Faye said, in case Connor would not know that and imagined the bees were zooming freely around the room. "You're scared," she observed, but she shut the door anyway.

To Evan's amused grin and Faye's neutral but curious expression, Connor explained, "I'm allergic."

"Sure," Evan drawled.

Connor did not react, so Evan dropped the taunts. "Did you see the beekeeper suits?"

"Uh-huh," Faye answered. "Five of them. But we don't know how many were there originally."

"What?" Connor asked.

"It's another legend about the shelter. Some insane person roams around underground in a beekeeper suit and with a smoke gun full of poisonous gas."

"Like Sandy Meade." Connor, too, had heard that infamous legend.

"It could be Sandy," Evan acknowledged. "Or it could be her killer. The rumor is he crawled in here from the sewers when the shelter was being built. It could be why the shelter has bees but no plants."

Marcus frowned. "Then what do they pollinate?"

"Nothing. The Beekeeper bred them so that they serve him."

"That doesn't make sense."

"There are always gaps in these kinds of legends," Faye explained.

"So, both Sandy Meade and the Beekeeper kill anyone who comes into the shelter?" Connor said.

"You know, a lot of legends are created as warning or lessons," Evan said.

"What's the lesson?"

"'Don't go into the shelter.'"

"Great."

Chapter 8

They found the cafeteria nearby. Though the room was brightly lit, the mustard yellow table covers leeched off some of the room's cheeriness. Faye thought the room looked more like a morgue than a school lunchroom.

The fact that several CPR dummies lay on top of some of the longer tables probably aided that impression.

The cafeteria adjoined the kitchen. No food lay out in the open, but trays were piled up at the entrance of the serving area, and silverware lay bundled in rolled cloth napkins. The silver surfaces gleamed with their suggestion of space-age futurism. Evan opened some of the cupboards, which contained canned goods and powdered milk. Several gaps appeared in the tight stacks of food, or so Evan and Marcus reported when they returned to the cafeteria.

Faye braved sitting with the dummies so she could monitor both the guys in the kitchen and Connor in the hallway, because he was not that interested in what was in the kitchen.

"Anything interesting happen?" Evan asked Faye.

"Not really."

Evan shifted his eyes at Connor in the hallway. He asked, in a low voice by her ear, "Do you think Leann's still down here?"

Faye wanted to say no. If she said no, he and Marcus could head up to the normal world, and she would only have to deal with convincing Connor.

"You can go back upstairs if you want to," she reminded him.

"We're not splitting up." Evan did not mean Connor. He meant Faye and Marcus and himself.

"I'll be fine."

Evan's mouth solidified into a firm frown. "Why do you want to help him?"

"I don't," Faye told him. She did not want to help Connor. She wanted him not to need help. She wanted Leann to quit playing hide-and-seek so they could all go back upstairs. She wanted the exploration of this shelter to be fun and not dependent on her classmates' secrets. More people complicated everything with their problems.

"But you will," Evan sighed. "We're not splitting up."

The room jolted violently. Faye, Evan, and Marcus ducked under the tables while Connor braced himself at the entrance. "Get under the table!"

Faye screamed at him, then flicked her eyes at Evan. *See what I mean? He's utterly helpless on his own.*

Connor slid under the nearest tables as the lights snapped out.

Several long minutes later, the floor settled still, and the overhead ceiling lights powered back to their full brightness.

"Um," Evan pointed Faye's attention to the side of the long table. Se CPR dummy had landed on its forehead so that the flapped face stared at them. "How did that happen?" The dummy had lain face-up on the table—it would have had to twist around its body during the quake.

"Everyone okay?" Marcus asked. Three "yeahs" answered.

Faye and Evan pushed themselves out first. Though some loose items had slid around, they saw no damage to the walls or ceiling.

"What was that?" Connor gawped as he straightened up and gave the room the same cursory glance.

"An earthquake," Marcus volunteered.

"Earthquakes don't happen here."

"They can. We're close to the New Madrid fault." To Evan, he gravely advised, "We'd better go back."

Connor predictably reminded them, "We need to find Leann."

"Searching for her won't do any good if we're trapped down here, too," Evan argued. "Let's at least make sure we have an exit."

Marcus woke up his phone. "We can get to the entrance quickly if we cut through this hallway. Come on."

Evan started to lead them out, but just as he reached the cafeteria door, a small figure pounced in front of him. Evan thrust up his hand at the last second to cover his body as the figure plunged its knife into him.

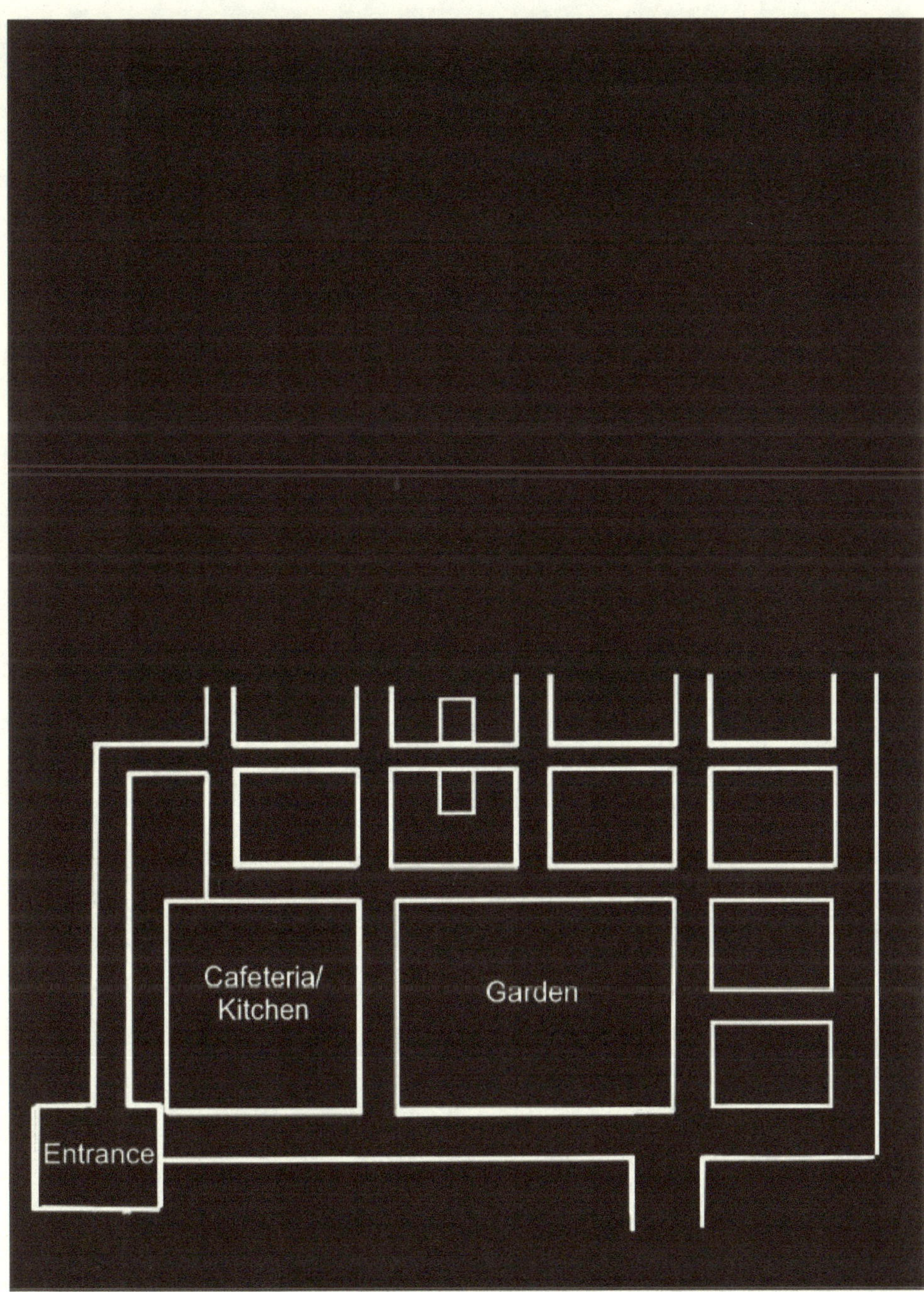
Cafeteria/
Kitchen
Garden
Entrance

Chapter 9

"I caught them!" a shrill voice yelled. "I caught the looters!"

Blood plopped onto the floor as Evan bent down, clutching his hand. Marcus started to dig for his first aid kit, but first found his extra fleece jacket. He used that to wrap the wound.

More footsteps hurried toward them. One of the strangers, a woman, ordered, "Betty, go get Roederer." Once she turned on the hall light, she reassessed the situation. "On second thought, Imogene should go. We might need your medical skills."

A girl their age nodded solemnly, while the younger girl with the knife skittered off in the opposite direction.

"Don't run!" The woman called at the girl before she sternly looked over the visitors. Her gaze rested on Connor for a moment, but she got over her inexplicable surprise quickly. "I want all of you against the wall here."

"Are you kidding?" Connor voiced.

"Betty," the woman said. Betty approached Faye, looking apologetic as she took the handcuffs from the woman and snapped them on Faye's wrist. The woman was rougher with Connor and Marcus.

"Why are you arresting us?" Evan hissed through gritted teeth. "We aren't the ones running around stabbing people."

"We take theft seriously," the woman explained, her tone implying that he should know that.

"We're just looking," Marcus said meekly.

Betty picked up the sunflower seeds Evan had pocketed.

"Thanks a lot, Newport," Connor muttered.

Imogene returned with a broad-muscled man. "Well, I'll be," he said philosophically.

"This one"—the woman pinched at Evan's uninjured arm—"should go to the infirmary, but I want the others in my office."

Faye spoke up. "He's not going alone."

The woman surveyed the group once more before she pointed at Marcus. "This one looks like he'll cause the least trouble."

Before they left, Roederer snatched the phone out of Marcus's hand. Marcus mouthed an attempt to protest. The guard examined the screen with a befuddled expression before tucking it into his shirt pocket. "Let's go."

Chapter 10

Faye and Connor were marched into her office, with knife-happy Imogene bringing up the rear. The teacher motioned for them to sit on the two chairs facing her desk. A name placard, Mrs. Standicliffe, offered her name so Faye and Connor did not have to ask.

"I want to know how you got in here," Mrs. Standicliffe ordered.

"The shelter door," Faye answered simply.

"That would be impossible. The door was designed to keep outsiders from breaking in once it was sealed."

"Then it wasn't sealed." Faye quickly ran through her memories of that morning. Did Connor know about the key? No way did she want these strangers learning about the key, and keeping that secret would go much easier if Connor did not know.

"That would be impossible."

"Then how do you think it happened?" Connor burst out.

Imogene stepped forward, pointing her knife at Connor. "That is not necessary, Imogene," Mrs. Standicliffe said, waving her back. "I'm sure you and your friends have sneaked in through the unfinished section."

"There's an unfinished section?" Faye asked. Evan would be overjoyed to hear that, which may or may not be a good thing.

"Don't—" Connor lost the words of whatever he wanted to say to her. He turned back to Mrs. Standicliffe. "Look, we go to the high school. She and her loverboy got the bright idea to explore here and find Sandy Meade—"

The woman's mouth tightened into a strange grimace at hearing the name. "There is no Sandy Meade here. I know all one hundred seventeen residents in this shelter." She laid her hands on the desk and leaned forward, trying to appear threatening or authoritative, but anyone could see that the mention of Sandy Meade had shaken her.

"You knew her," Faye said. The older generations at Haven Point did not like to admit to knowing Sandy Meade. The former students who would have grown up with her had formed a deliberate amnesia of any personal interaction with her. Evan had tried many times to interview them for their memories, but not one of them budged from their firm denials.

"Who's Sandy Meade?" Imogene asked.

The administrator ignored her question. "I would still like to get an explanation about where you come from. A family bunker, I suppose."

"No. We come from the real world, not some sci-fi theme park," Connor said in his usual tactless manner.

Mrs. Standicliffe squinted her eyes at them. She rotated her chair to the shelves behind her and picked out the last volume in the top row, which she then spread open at the edge of her desk so that both Connor and Faye could also see what was on the pages. It was a yearbook.

"Austin Barrows' son, right?" Mrs. Standicliffe identified.

"Yes." Connor's voice turned wary.

Imogene leaned over the desk, her curious eyes drinking in the photos. "There's my mom and dad," she said, pointing with her finger this time. Steven Barter and Lisa Basso had been placed next to each other by virtue of the alphabet. "They didn't even meet until after the war. Isn't that fizzy?" She looked up at Connor. "Is your mom in here, too?"

"No," Connor said gruffly. "She went to Prestville."

"Where's that?" Which only added more bizarreness to the interrogation. Prestville was about a thirty-minute drive from Haven Point—someone at Haven Point asking where Prestville was located was like someone from Staten Island asking where Manhattan was.

Mrs. Standicliffe interceded. "Imogene, sit down." She tried to soften her facial expression. "You must understand, we have not heard of any local survivors until today."

"What about the looters?" Faye asked.

"We haven't had any other looters." Imogene bounced forward. "You're the first looters we ever caught, and I was the one to catch you. That'll make me famous." To Mrs. Standicliffe, she asked, "Are we going to execute them?"

"Imogene, one more outburst and your curfew moves up to seven thirty for the rest of the year." Imogene immediately quieted. Back to Connor and Faye, the older woman said, "I would like to know more about the other survivors in the area. Maybe we could make arrangements to meet with your father?" she asked, with a blast of youthful hope.

"I can't," Connor said shortly. "He died four years ago."

"I see." Mrs. Standicliffe looked wistfully down at the yearbook.

Only Faye seemed aware of the division of reality between the two groups. Imogene had babbled about her strange history of a war and looters, and Mrs. Standicliffe asked about bunkers and brought up the yearbook like it was relevant to the fact that they had just caught four intruders in their cafeteria. Yet, Mrs. Standicliffe knew Connor's father and recognized Sandy Meade's name.

Faye hesitated to mention any of these peculiarities. Mrs. Standicliffe all but declared that people lived down here. One hundred seventeen people, to be exact. (One hundred eighteen, if she counted Sandy Meade.) Which only raised more questions. Like why? What did they believe had happened to the world above?

Not that Faye was going to voice these questions. When it came right down to it, Mrs. Standicliffe did not have to explain anything to them. This was her place, and Faye and Connor were the intruders. Asking questions that pointed out their intruder status would not do them any favors.

Faye would have to put up with everyone tiptoeing around these mismatched histories until someone else noticed, preferably Mrs. Standicliffe or one of the other residents they had just discovered.

Chapter 11

While Betty cleaned and stitched up Evan's hand, Roederer played with the phone, examining it with fascination.

"What is this?" he asked.

"It's a phone," Marcus answered. He did not add anything else to his explanation. Evan and Faye might not have believed it, but he could be discreet, too.

"Why does a phone need a TV screen?"

"Because it does other things."

"Like what?"

"Internet access, music, games." Marcus purposely left out "camera" as one of its functions, because something about this place resembled a secret military base.

"Where did you get it?" Roederer asked.

"Best Buy"

"What's that?"

"It must be what they call their market on the surface," Betty answered gently.

"Cool." The comment had Marcus reassess Roederer's age. He looked to be in his early twenties—twenty-five at the oldest.

Betty clipped the thread. "You'll have to have your medic examine the wound in a day or so."

"Okay." Evan had trouble finding something clever to say to the girl, who had the air of an efficient nurse in one of those World War II dramas that his grandmother loved to watch. Betty was a lot better looking—okay, hotter—than any nurse he had ever seen in real life.

A bell sounded. Marcus visibly jumped. "What's that?"

"The first morning bell," Betty explained. "For the residents that have breakfast duty."

"Wait a minute." Marcus powered the phone on briefly. It was close to nine o' clock. What military unit waited until nine o' clock in the morning to start breakfast?

"It's a clock, too," Roederer announced.

"It gives the wrong time," Betty said, peering over Marcus' shoulder. "It's three hours ahead."

"That's not right." Marcus frowned. "Evan, what does your phone say?"

"Faye broke it, remember?"

"Connor broke it." Though Marcus would never dare say that if Connor were in the room.

"Faye's more likely to pay for a replacement," Evan reasoned.

"That sounds . . . exploitative."

"Do Faye and her boyfriend have clock phones, too?" Betty asked.

"He's not her boyfriend," Evan said, willing that horrifying image to disappear quickly from his head. "Speaking of which, there was someone else who came down here. About five foot six, shoulder-length brown hair, blue eyes, dark blue jacket?"

Betty shook her head. Roederer looked confused, like he did not want to admit out loud how badly he failed at his guarding the halls.

"Were you guarding the halls alone?" Evan asked.

"No. I was with Lyle and Tanner. We had our eyes on the screens until Imogene ran in."

"Screens?"

"I don't like them either," Betty confessed, "but they only show the hallways, and we only run the cameras at night."

As far as you know, Evan wanted to retort. But instead, he asked incredulously, "And you didn't see us at all? We were in the hallways a lot of the time."

"You're confessing to that?" Roederer asked, equally incredulous.

"We didn't know anyone was down here. Besides Leann. We were just exploring."

"And stealing sunflower seeds," Betty reminded him.

"I didn't know they belonged to anyone." Okay, maybe the cleanliness of the halls and bathrooms should have clued him in that the shelter had not been as abandoned as he had believed. "But you have them back. I can throw in a bag of trail mix as a gesture of good faith, if you want." Evan bent over his backpack and started sorting through his items. Roederer eagerly looked over his shoulder.

Evan handed Betty the trail mix. It was a prepackaged kind. She pinched the cellophane between her fingers.

The floor jerked from under them. *This again*, Evan thought. No tables to shelter under this time, so Evan and Marcus moved to the corner with the least furniture. Betty knelt under the tray—it was not going to protect her if the ceiling caved, Evan knew, so he hoped that did not happen. Roederer stayed by the backpack, not really bothered enough to take cover.

After a few seconds, it ended. Several of Betty's utensils, including a pair of scissors, had fallen off the tray. Betty quickly gathered them up and sealed them in a cloth bag.

"Was that a bomb?" Roederer asked casually.

"It was an earthquake," Marcus corrected. He began to inform them about the New Madrid fault.

Roederer jumped in on the first available pause. "Wait, why would someone build a bomb shelter on a fault line?"

"We aren't exactly on the fault line," Marcus admitted. "But if another earthquake hit with the same intensity as the one in 1812, we would definitely feel it."

"I have never heard of this." Betty stood, squeezing her hands together.

"Maybe Mrs. S has," Roederer suggested.

"Or Mr. Dennis."

Marcus only shook his head sorrowfully. *Sorry that he could not get a signal so he could not pull up any informative articles from the Internet*, Evan guessed.

"We should reconvene with the others," Roederer declared.

Chapter 12

When they left the nurse's office, the halls were dark and quiet. Roederer charged ahead, but Betty hesitated. As she closed the door behind them, she gripped the doorknob so it rattled in her shaking hand.

"It's quiet," she said.

They snaked the halls to the TV monitors room. Roederer burst open the door.

"Holy biscuits."

The tangy smell of blood hit Evan's nose, so he could already guess what he would see before he peeked in. Two men sat in their wooden chairs, their heads turned so they faced the ceiling, exposing their slit throats.

Roederer buckled to his knees and vomited onto the floor. After wiping his mouth, he remembered Betty. "Betty, don't come in here." But Betty had already seen it. She froze, her eyes glazed over like a deer noticing a speeding car barreling toward it.

"Find Mrs. S?" Marcus said shallowly. It seemed like the logical next step.

Evan did not remember them stampeding toward the main offices, or what was said to Mrs. S and Faye, or colliding into the floor. The next scene he was aware of, he was lying on the floor of the office, and Mrs. Standicliffe was talking into an intercom and frowning because she was not getting anyone to respond.

"Betty said it was blood loss," Faye reassured him as he sat up. Faye and Connor were the most composed in the room, not having seen or known the victims. Lyle and Tanner. Why did Roederer have to say their names? Evan would have preferred never knowing their names.

"Did you do anything to the communication systems?" Mrs. Standicliffe accused wildly.

"No," Marcus answered. "It could have been the earthquake. I can try the police." Extracting his phone, he dialed 911, but the call did not seem to be getting through.

"The police?" Mrs. Standicliffe shrieked.

"They were the police, dodo-head." Imogene took it upon herself to explain.

"Maybe you should put that down," Faye suggested, because Imogene was still waving her knife around, and it could not have been helping anyone overcome the shock.

"If I put it away, you'll escape."

"We're still handcuffed."

"That is it!" Mrs. Standicliffe shouted. "We're going to have to check downstairs."

"That's a bad idea," Evan mumbled.

She whirled around. "Why?"

"Because instead of roaming around the hallways like slasher movie fodder, we should stay here and find some way to alert someone outside the shelter."

"The morning shifts will be starting shortly," Roederer reminded her. "All we have to do is wait for them to find us here."

"But the students . . ." Mrs. Standicliffe gasped.

"Would anyone try to attack them in the crowded hallways?" Roederer's question betrayed uncertainty.

Three quarters of the room jumped when the bell rang.

"The breakfast bell," Betty identified flatly for the newcomers.

They listened for noises outside the room.

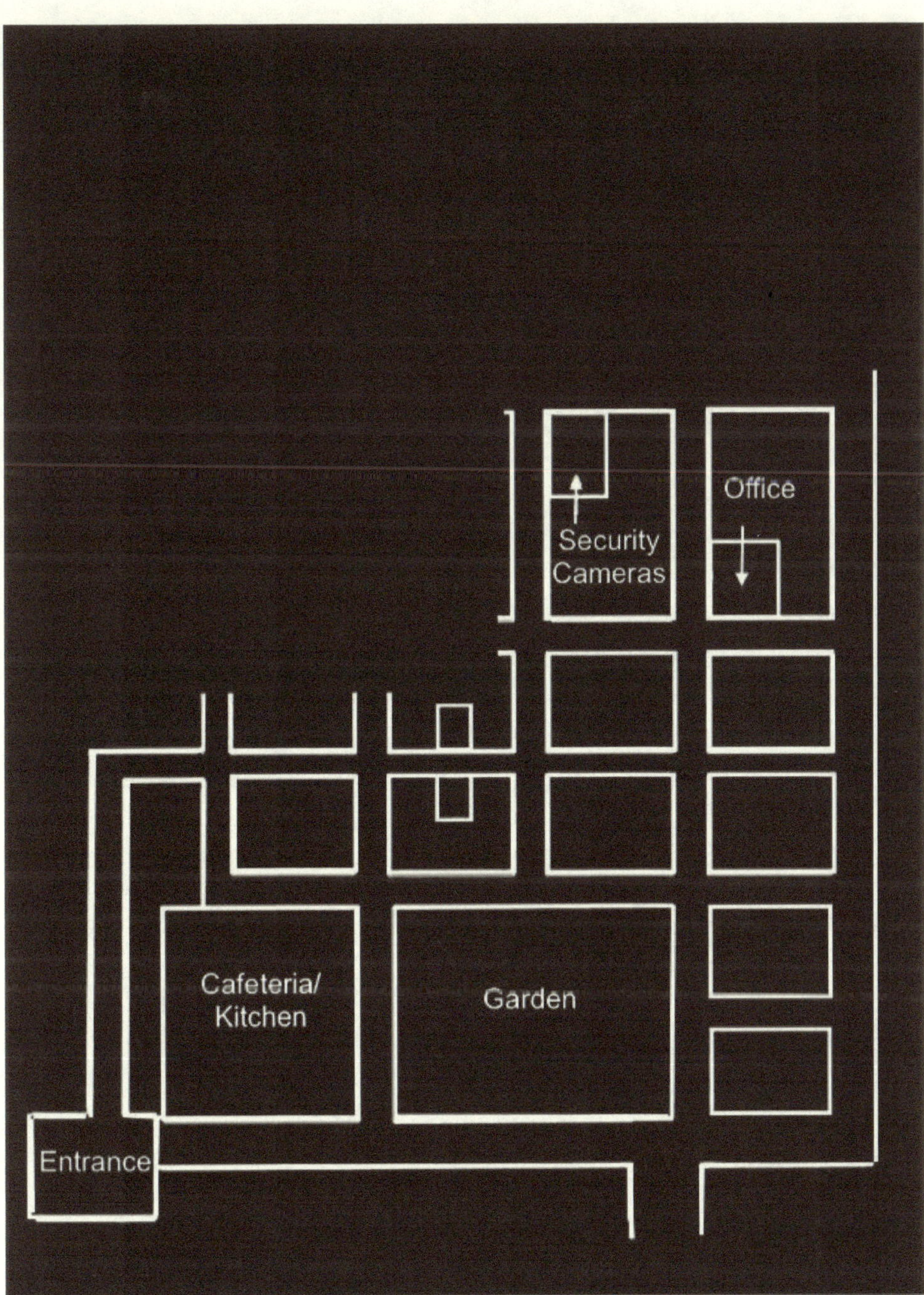
Office
Security
Cameras
Cafeteria/
Kitchen
Garden
Entrance

Chapter 13

Faye discerned no difference in the noise level from when they had first entered the shelter. By the increasing confusion she saw on the expressions of Mrs. Standicliffe and Roederer, she could only assume that it was unusual for the halls to be so quiet at this time of day.

Gone was any professional stance from Mrs. Standicliffe. Her hair, which she had tucked up in a neat bun, now descended in frizzy tangles around her shoulders. There was something vaguely familiar, vaguely adolescent, about the way she gnawed at her thumbnail.

Faye glanced back at the yearbooks. She would bet Mrs. Standicliffe's picture would show up on one of those pages as a clueless but hope-filled teen. A classmate of Austin Barrows and Imogene's parents.

And Sandy Meade's.

"May I see the yearbook again?" she asked Imogene.

"Why?"

"I want to see some people in it."

Imogene glared suspiciously at her, but she was also curious about what Faye might know. She picked up the yearbook with her free hand and set it in front of Faye, who slid to the floor and knelt at the side of her chair so she could reach the pages. She turned forward until she reached the Mc–Me section for the juniors.

"Evan," she hissed.

Evan snapped his head up. He looked like he had zoned out for a minute or so. He needed something to drink to make up for the blood loss. "What?"

"Sandy Meade's picture is here."

Mrs. Standicliffe snatched the yearbook away from her. "Have some respect for the dead," she scolded.

"Is she dead?" Faye asked.

"She's not here." As if that answered the question by itself.

"Who is she?" Imogene asked.

"She went to school here," Faye explained.

"Before the war?"

"Yep."

"Was she a friend of Mrs. Standicliffe's?"

"Why are you doing this?" The older woman's fear surfaced once again. "Sandy Meade has nothing to do with this! She isn't here!"

"Great idea, Faye. Let's make the crazy lady crazier," Connor grumbled.

Marcus nervously eyed Mrs. Standicliffe as he whispered as quietly as he could, "You think she could have . . .?"

Roederer instantly picked up on what Marcus was hinting. "Why would this girl want to kill my colleagues?" he asked.

Connor answered before Faye or Marcus could weave their stories. "There's this stupid rumor that she's a ghost out to kill everyone who bullied her."

Roederer let out an abrupt laugh. "Ghosts don't exist. If they did, this place would be packed with them."

"How do you know about her?" Betty asked Connor, slowly coming out of her shocked state.

"Told you. Stupid ghost story."

"It's more logical for the killer to be one of you," Betty said.

"Why would we do that?" Connor asked, exasperated.

"Because they caught you stealing."

"For one packet of sunflower seeds?"

"Maybe you intended to steal more, but Imogene stopped you."

"Yeah, I did." Imogene smiled.

Roederer shook his head sternly. "Someone should have been here by now."

"What if they're all dead?" Imogene asked.

"They are not dead," Mrs. Standicliffe broke in weakly. She edged toward the door handle and flung it open. Dark, empty hallways met her, but that did not stop her from running out.

Before Roederer trooped out after her, he hastily ordered, "Stay here and keep the door shut. Put some furniture in front. Don't let anyone in except Mrs. S or myself." Then he, too, disappeared.

"Goodbye, adult authority figures," Evan mumbled.

As Betty grabbed Mrs. S's chair to jam in front of the door, Marcus searched through his pack and pulled out a water bottle and a sugary flavor mix. "Drink this," he said, shoving the bottle of pink liquid at Evan. Evan grabbed the bottle and took a swig.

"How long will your food last?" Betty asked.

"Two or three days," Marcus answered.

"We are not going to wait here two or three days," Connor said. "I say we make a dash for the entrance."

"And leave Mrs. S and Roederer?" Betty asked.

"If they're smart, they'll go to the entrance, too."

"What about Leann?" Evan asked.

"Who's Leann?" Betty asked. "Another ghost?"

"You didn't tell them about Leann?" Evan repeated to Faye and Connor.

"We were getting to it," Faye answered. "We had a lot of weirdness to cover." To Betty and Imogene, she summed up, "A friend of ours got separated from us earlier."

"She's the killer!" Imogene declared.

"She's not the killer." Connor aimed a warning glare at Evan against fueling more of everyone's imaginative theories. "The police will look for anyone still in here."

"How many live on the surface?" Betty asked.

"The surface of what?"

"How many live above ground?" she tried to clarify. "Mrs. S and the others didn't think there were any survivors on the surface. They wouldn't last long in the radiation unless they had a shelter like ours."

"Wait, wait, wait!" Evan sputtered. "You're saying you've never been above ground?"

Betty's cheeks turned pink. Imogene only tilted her head, looking at them as if they had grown horns.

"Nobody has. Except for Mrs. S and Mr. Dennis and other old people."

"That's messed up," Evan could not help but comment.

"This is the one of the safest places to live since the war," Betty defended. "We have food and water, clothes, and medicine. We get to go to school and keep a garden. Our lives are as normal as they possibly can be. You must have seen much worse, living on the surface."

"True," Faye agreed.

Evan rubbed his forehead, trying to figure what these girls were doing here in the first place. They *lived* down here? This was messed up. Violation-of-human-rights level messed up.

"What is this war you keep talking about?" he asked. He was pretty sure, by now, that this "war" had never happened. Mrs. S and the others had lied about it to keep them down here for some reason. Social experiment? Or was

Mrs. S just part of a team of insane psychopaths that got off on trapping kids underground?

"Didn't your parents tell you about the Commies? The Commies bombed us," Imogene said.

"We don't know that, Imogene." Betty looked at Evan to ascertain if that was true.

"We weren't bombed," Evan said.

"Mrs. S was there when the bombs fell," Imogene claimed. "She told us about it a lot. She was at a school dance, and the sirens went off, and people ran to the shelter. She told us about the ground shaking, and they had to shut the door when the air got hot, even though not everybody was inside."

"That's all wrong," Evan said. "The country didn't get bombed. The Cold War ended. They took down the Berlin Wall in 1989, and the Soviet Union crumbled in 1991. Mrs. S lied to you!"

"Mrs. S heard the bombs," Imogene said.

The room fell silent.

The faint sound of footsteps emanated from the other side of the door. Betty crouched by the door to listen. Marcus leaned next to her.

"Is it Roederer?" Imogene whispered. Betty shook her head.

The footsteps stopped. A louder scrape came through, then another, then another, like something clawing into the wood. Nobody in the room moved or called out, and there was no window for anyone to peer through. The scrapes ended, and the person at the door walked away.

Faye connected with Connor's hand. "Leann?" she mouthed when he looked over. He jerked his head slightly from side to side to say no.

"She's gone," Marcus said.

"Are you sure it was a girl?" Evan asked.

"We know it wasn't Roederer."

"No, it was your ghost," Connor sneered.

"I don't see you going out there to find out who that was," Evan said.

Several minutes later, Roederer pounded on the door. As they had not set up any special code beforehand, he announced himself by yelling, "It's Roederer! Open up!"

Betty and Marcus pulled out the chair and opened the door.

"What happened?" Roederer asked. He pushed the door completely open so they could see the word UGLEANN carved into the wood.

"Who wrote that on the door? What's an ug-leen?"

Chapter 14

Everyone started to pour out of the office, except Faye and Connor, who were still restrained. "Hey, handcuffs," Connor reminded them.

Roederer found the key and unlocked Faye's wrist first, then Connor's.

"I couldn't find Mrs. S," he explained quickly. "Then I went downstairs. Everyone's disappeared."

"Disappeared? Like the Rapture?" Faye asked.

"I don't know. I didn't see blood or anything. They just weren't there."

"What's downstairs?" Evan wanted to know.

"The dorms." Roederer's answer was so ridiculously ordinary that both Evan and Marcus looked slightly ashamed for building up so much fear with their imaginations when they saw the stairs.

"We should go back above ground," Evan proposed once more. "The police can find Mrs. S."

"These people think the bombs never happened," Imogene told Roederer.

"Huh? Of course they happened."

"They said Mrs. S lied about the surface getting bombed."

"Uh-uh. There were bombs."

"Did you see it happen?" Evan challenged.

"Before my time. But we got bombed. We wouldn't have been down here all this time if we hadn't."

"How about we go back to the surface, and you guys stay down here?" Connor suggested. "That way, everyone's happy."

Everyone ignored him.

"What if there weren't any bombs?" Betty said.

"The teachers wouldn't lie about something like that," Roederer stubbornly defended.

"There have been bigger lies in history," Evan pointed out.

"What if we're both right?" Marcus said.

"This isn't *Doctor Who*," Connor muttered, foreseeing what Marcus was going to suggest.

"What is he talking about?" Betty asked.

"We're from two different universes," Marcus said. "The earthquakes shifted us to your universe or you to ours."

The theory did not compute with Roederer and the girls. Evan had to remind himself that they had not spent their lives rotting their brains with science fiction tropes. He tried to think of a relevant title that predated the eighties. "It's like that story where these people go back in time, and they aren't supposed to touch anything because the smallest change could alter the future in terrible ways, but that one guy accidentally steps on that bug—"

"We traveled back in time?" Roederer asked.

"What story is this?" Betty wanted to know.

"It's by Ray Bradbury. Anyway, the characters go back to the present time —"

"We only have *The Martian Chronicles*." Betty's eyes showed a glint of excitement. "You have more of his books?"

"I'm going to the entrance," Connor announced. "The rest of you can stand around and discuss sci-fi books until the person who carved into the door comes back."

"Oh, biscuits," Roederer said. "Back into the office."

"No, I'm leaving."

"I wanna go with," Imogene whined. "I'll just stab any looters if they try to mess with us."

Betty pulled Imogene back. "No, you're not running off with strangers."

"If we get to the shelter entrance, we can call the police from there," Faye explained. "If we're in our world," she added for Marcus's benefit.

"I guess we can't wait in the office forever," Evan conceded. If what Roederer had said about the others disappearing was true, no one would be coming to find them. For all he knew, Ruby and everyone above could have disappeared, too. "We either have to contact someone outside or find out who killed the guards. I'm guessing that you don't have a lot of experience in nabbing killers, so we'll go with the first option."

They progressed past two classrooms when a voice called out from a darkened hallway, one that Marcus had not yet mapped. "Connor? Evan? Where are you?"

Chapter 15

Roederer whipped toward the sound of the voice."Who's that?"

"I can't move," the voice pleaded.

Connor took off down the hall. "Lee?"

"I'm scared."

Betty started following behind him. "Are you hurt?" she shouted to the unknown voice.

"There's blood. I don't know where the blood came from."

They turned the corner. The massive door to a gymnasium glinted ahead of them. A muffled clank sounded from off to the side and behind them, where a narrow set of elevator doors were located.

Connor snapped on his own flashlight just in time to witness the metal doors opening. They revealed Leann, slumped in the blood-smeared interior.

Betty ducked in to touch the girl's wrist. "She's alive. Go to the gym and find a pallet so we can carry her out."

"On it." Evan pulled Faye's sleeve, and they sprinted across to the gym. They opened the doors.

The gym floor was covered with CPR dummies lying on pallets. Nearly all of them were butchered or deformed in some grotesque fashion.

"This is . . ." For once, words failed Evan. He bent to one of the pallets, and gently pushed the dummy off. As he did so, he saw a name etched in the pallet.

"Her name is Nicole," he blurted out.

Faye glanced at the dummy behind her. "Looks like they all have names." She helped Evan heft up the pallet, and they carried it to the elevator. It fit, barely, in the narrow space, and Betty and Faye stepped around the edges to prop Leann onto the pallet and pull her out.

"Do we take her back to the nurse's office?" Evan asked.

"That's more equipped for minor injuries," Betty said. "There's a bigger infirmary on the lower level, but getting her there will be risky if whatever hurt her is down there. Mrs. S said that just after the bombs fell, they put the injured people in the gym."

"That might not be a good idea," Evan said.

Marcus had unearthed his emergency kit and opened it for the others to examine. "Is there anything you need that we don't have here?"

"I should wash the scrape on her head so it doesn't get infected. And towels. Clean towels. Cleaner than . . ."

"Locker room?" Faye suggested, and Betty nodded.

Faye ran to the nearest locker room, paying no attention to which gender it had been designated for. She rifled through the office to find another kit, some towels, and a blanket. She had no idea if the blanket was clean enough or not, but she folded it between the stack of towels and her own chest, then trundled out.

"There's a bed in there," she told them.

"The gym would be easier to secure," Roederer said.

"Great idea, if you want her to die of shock once she wakes up and finds herself surrounded by creepy dummies," Evan muttered.

"What?" Connor asked, having been unable to add any helpful input after he found Leann in her current condition.

"We'll move the dummies," Marcus said. "He's right. In the gym we'll be able to see what's around us. Someone could have been hiding and jumped out on Faye when she was in the locker room. She shouldn't have gone in there alone."

Faye said nothing. She did not know for sure that she had been alone in the locker room. She had not been looking for attackers.

Evan gave in. "Fine. Creepy gym it is."

Everyone except Betty was visibly startled as they entered. Betty was too concerned about Leann's condition to notice. The others started dragging pallets far away from the corner they staked out as theirs.

Betty took a smaller towel and a bottle of water and wiped at the wound. "It's not as bad as it looks," she said.

"She lost a lot of blood," Connor said doubtfully.

"I don't think all that blood was hers," Roederer mentioned.

"Could it be Mrs. S?" Imogene guessed.

"No."

"Possibly," Roederer answered at the same time as Connor. "Mrs. S was panicked. If she ran into your friend, she wouldn't have recognized her. They might have fought."

"Hey, someone sliced this one's throat open," Imogene called from halfway across the room as she bent over one of the more grotesquely mutilated dummies.

"We noticed," Evan said crossly.

"And this one has its skull cracked open. And these dummies over here —they're burned." She wrinkled her nose. "Really burned."

"Does anyone else know how to look for signs of concussions?" Betty asked. "If so, one of us needs to stay awake for the next twenty-four hours to watch her."

"This one's melted to goo."

"Hey, Imogene, don't go in there," Roederer called, just as the girl disappeared into the far corner behind the bleachers.

"Want me to go get her?" Faye asked.

"So you can disappear, too," Evan balked. "Great idea."

"I'll go with her," Roederer said. "We need a third person."

Evan glanced around. Betty and Marcus were tending to Leann, and Connor was not about to separate from his girlfriend. "Figures."

Chapter 16

Roederer entered the darkened room first and flicked on the lights. A locker room identical to the one Faye had raided appeared, mazelike with its banks of lockers and shower stalls. To complicate things, the lockers looked large enough for a girl Imogene's size to fit into without much discomfort.

A shower ran full blast. Clouds of steam emanated from the bank of stalls and humidified the room, making a rather distinctive difference in temperature from the bleakly lit and chilly gym.

Could Imogene have activated the motion sensors? Evan reconsidered the question. *Were there motion sensors?* If not, Imogene could just as easily have toggled with one of the shower heads, but Evan could not figure out what purpose that would serve.

"You watch the back," Roederer instructed Evan. He inched along the wall, checking between each row of lockers before he moved on. They rounded the corner and approached the steaming shower.

"I can go first," Faye offered.

"No." Roederer set down his flashlight and took off his outer uniform shirt. He wrapped the shirt around his face to provide a little bit of a shield, with enough visor space to allow him to see. He stepped to the edge of the bank of shower stalls.

The steam shrouded the flesh-colored form underneath the farthest shower spout. Roederer started to inch toward it.

Evan had been watching the back and Faye the side, but they could not tell exactly where the attacker appeared from. Its rubbery arms latched onto Evan and dragged him back. Roederer fell forward into the scalding water.

Faye had fallen out of the blast's range. She grabbed Roederer's ankles and pulled him out of the stall. By the time she had gotten him out of danger, Evan had disappeared, and so had the figure that claimed him.

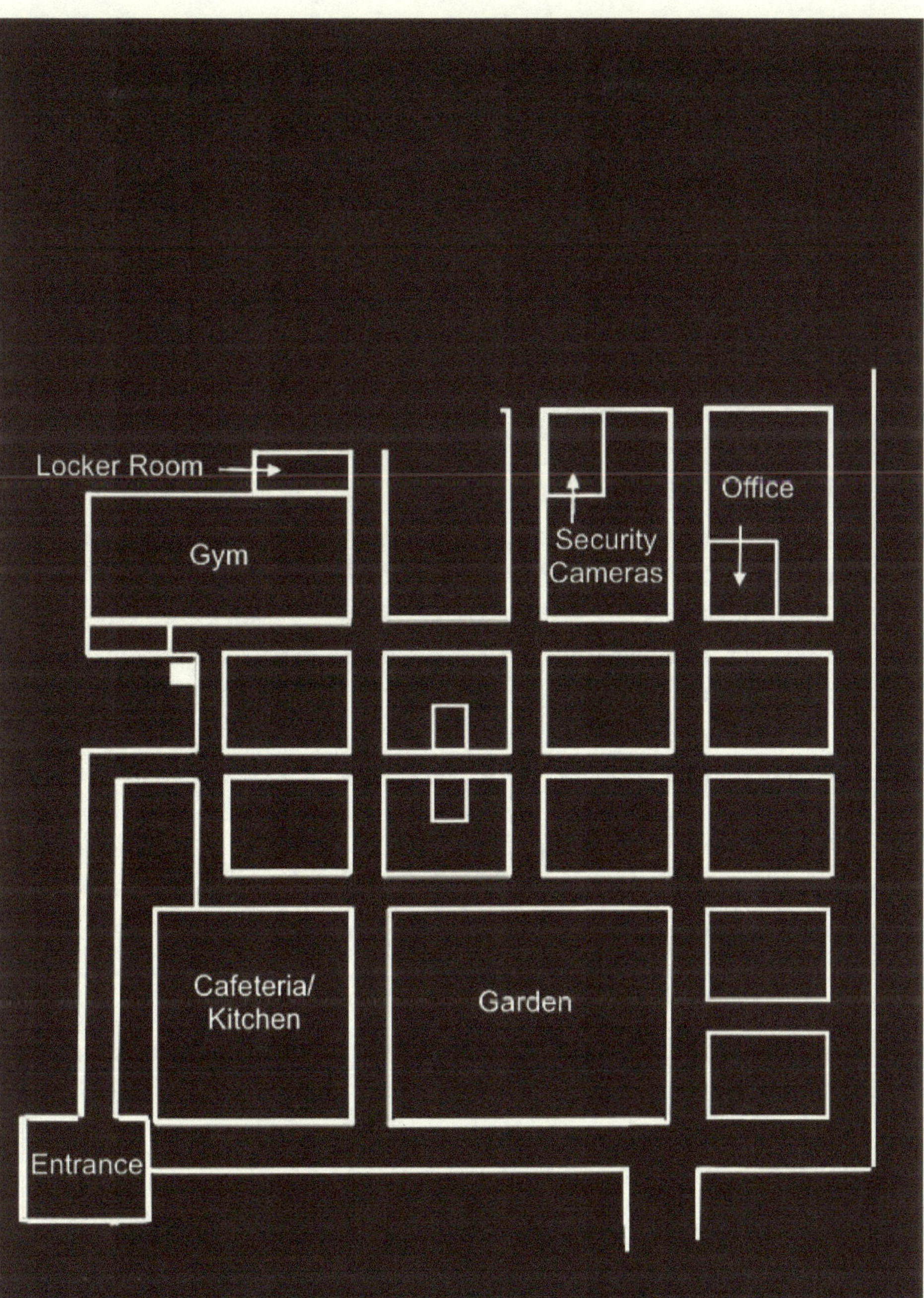
Locker Room
Office
Security
Cameras
Gym
Cafeteria/
Kitchen
Garden
Entrance

Chapter 17

Connor hurried in when he heard the screams. "What happened?"

"He's burned," Faye said. "Evan got taken by someone."

"We'll have to get Betty."

Roederer's howls of pain subsided. He lay still, his hands covering his eyes.

Betty stumbled in between them. "Remove his belt and pants. Not his shirt. It's been grafted into his skin. We need clean, lukewarm water," she said, clearly doing her best to contain her stress.

Faye searched through her backpack and pulled out her very large water bottle. Evan's backpack had disappeared with him; not that it mattered because his water was probably useless with the crystal sugar stuff in it. She passed her bottle to Betty.

Roederer jerked as Betty dribbled the water around his face. She waited for him to settle before she unwound the towel. Roederer's face was peeling, and his eyes winched shut.

The skin around his neck and on his upper arms had started to form bubbles of pus. Betty monitored his breathing but frowned grimly.

"Another pallet?" Connor guessed.

She nodded, tears springing to her eyes.

After Connor and Faye shoved one of the burned, gooey dummies off a pallet and brought it over, Betty laid out a towel on the pallet and tried to ease Roederer onto it. He remained on his side as Betty checked his eyes again, unsure if she should hope that he was conscious.

She turned to Faye. "Are you burned?"

"No."

Betty's concerned gaze fell down to the other girl's hands, which did not even look reddened.

They headed back to where Marcus waited with Leann.

"Where's Evan?" Marcus asked.

"Someone grabbed him," Faye explained. "Someone taller than Imogene. I don't know where she is, either. There was something in the shower, but none of us got a good look. It might have been another dummy," she suggested meekly. "I don't think it moved."

Marcus looked green. He thought maybe it was Imogene in the shower, and he was sure the same thought occurred to Faye.

"So much for everything being visible," Connor said.

Betty winced. "Imogene should have stayed with us. She knew not to wander off on her own."

"What about Evan?" Marcus asked. "How did he disappear?"

"Whoever grabbed him took him through a hidden door," Faye said. "I can find it."

"Are you suicidal or something?" Connor said.

"Do you have a better idea for getting Evan back?" Faye reasoned.

Connor could not say he did. Neither did Marcus, who fidgeted uneasily but did not chime in with Faye that they should go after him, nor Betty, who wore a guilty grimace because of Imogene's part in Evan's disappearance.

"Roederer had the same idea, and look what happened to him," Connor argued. He had to admit he was not thrilled with the idea of abandoning anyone to certain death, even someone as obnoxious as Evan Newport. He might as well be realistic, though. Faye should know how grim her chances of survival would be if she went after him.

"Okay, I'll look by myself." Faye stood up. "I don't want to risk anyone else's life, so don't come after me."

She marched off, past the dummies and through the shadowy door to the locker room.

The shower had stopped. Faye entered the shower banks and discovered that the figure that had been absorbing the steaming water was, in fact, a dummy mounted on a pole. Its rubber skin oozed into darkened holes that looked not that dissimilar to third-degree burns. That was one mystery solved, though she expected the "why" of it would remain unexplained.

Faye looked to the moist wall that adjoined the shower stall. A broader crack ran down along the wall. The line was thicker than the other tile borders. She rubbed her forefinger into the gap.

At that moment, a hand brushed at her upper arm.

Chapter 18

"You're suicidal," Connor accused, out of breath after chasing her across the gym. "That's the only thing that would explain why you would come back here."

"What does that make you?" Faye said, not really invested in the argument. She went back to examining the wall. Foregoing all caution, she pushed at the squares: lightly at first, then again with increasing force. The tile blocks yielded and swung open.

"What the—?" Connor did not know why anything else that they found in the shelter should surprise him.

Faye aimed her light through the doorway. Tiles nearly identical to the ones in the shower stall brightened within her beam. The room was cooler and smelled mustier. Drips plinked a steady monotone from a faucet out of her sight.

Faye stepped through the opening.

"Hey, where are you going?"

"To find Evan," Faye answered. She'd wasted enough time that could have been spent finding Evan, and she did not bother wasting more explaining that to Connor.

She hurried, and nearly tripped, out of the mirrorlike shower stall to discover a locker room devoid of lockers and benches and everything else except crumbled tiles and ceiling dust. Two doors presented at opposite ends of the room. Faye tried the door at the far right, but it held as tightly as if it had been cemented shut, so she went out the other door.

Endless hallways lengthened before her, and the doors appeared unnumbered and in rough shape. She swept her flashlight beam across the floor to check for wet footprints but found nothing.

"Faye," Connor tried to sound nice and reasonable. "Let's go back. You don't know which way they went."

"You can go back," Faye said. "I'm going to keep searching." She tried the door next to the one they had just traveled through. It swung open, revealing a nearly empty supply closet.

"I see. When it's your boyfriend that's missing, then it's fine to drop everything and run after him."

"We did drop everything to look for Leann. You wouldn't have known where to go if we hadn't gone with you," Faye reminded him.

"Do you know where you're going?""Better than you do."

They came upon a set of double doors leading to an auditorium. Faye yanked at the door handles and found they were latched shut. When she peered through the nearly opaque gray windows, she saw nothing but darkness inside.

Until a face popped up and pressed its cheek to the glass.

"Very funny, Imogene. Open up."

The face only smiled back before ducking out of sight. The lock clicked, and the door parted open. Imogene stepped out, showing only a bare trace of shame for her behavior.

"Evan's missing," Faye told her. "And Roederer's hurt. They were looking for you."

Imogene bounced on her heels. "So? If you didn't come here, none of this would be happening. Anyway, I was going to tell you I saw another looter."

She ran past, narrowly dodging Connor as he tried to block her from escaping. After running a good distance down the hall, she slowed down and looked back to see if the older teens were chasing after her.

"Don't you care about the looter? I bet it's another one of your friends."

"Did you see Evan? Or some person in a tan suit?" Faye asked.

"So he is your friend," Imogene accused back. "He's right behind you."

"She's joking, right?" Connor muttered, as if it were up to Faye to translate Imogene's craziness to him.

Faye looked anyway.

A figure wearing a beekeeper suit stood several yards away from them. Black netting obscured the face, and a gloved hand gripped a metal canister.

Now that it had their attention, the figure strode toward them.

Connor yanked at Faye's arm, and they raced down the hall after Imogene. Imogene rounded the corner and slipped through another entrance to the auditorium. She shut the door behind her and locked it, stranding Connor and Faye in the hall.

The Beekeeper had closed in on them, leaving them little more choice than to stumble along the hall. They had not gotten much farther before the figure reached out and yanked Faye back. "Run!" she yelled, but Connor was not about to leave her behind. He grabbed the closest weapon he could find

—a fire ax hanging on the wall—and aimed it at the figure's arm, hoping to disable it before it sprayed its canister.

At the same time, Faye tried to kick in the Beekeeper's kneecaps, but the Beekeeper kept a tight hold on her. It lifted her in the ax's path before Connor could stop it.

The blade planted itself into the back of Faye's skull.

Chapter 19

Connor let go of the ax, suddenly breathless. He barely noticed the Beekeeper escape after it dropped Faye into a crumpled heap on the floor. She landed facedown, with the ax handle protruding in the air. He did not want to see her like this—bloody and dead—but he could not look away.

He thought that branding Leann with that nickname years ago would be the worst thing he had ever done.

Then Faye sat up. Her arms snaked behind her. She gripped the ax handle and pulled the weapon out of her head.

"Next time I tell you to run, you run." She plunked the ax on the floor by her knees.

Faye rose to a stand and directed her flashlight around the hallway for any sign of the Beekeeper. "Where did he go?" she asked Connor.

"Connor?" She looked back, shining the light on his face. "Get up!"

Connor stared back, still dazed.

"Are you hurt?" Faye asked, as it had only at that moment occurred to her.

"No," Connor managed to choke out.

"Good. Did you see where the Beekeeper went?"

"No, I didn't!" Connor exploded. "I had just stuck an ax in your head!"

"It's out now." When that failed to console him, she said, "Don't worry about it. I don't die."

Connor still looked confused. "What does that mean?"

"Sere isn't much more to it." Faye did not have a special name to describe what she was exactly. Some human terms came close, but the mythology did not really get it right. "No tragic origin story or anything. That's just how I've been for centuries."

"Is Evan also a . . . what you are?"

"Not as far as I know." Faye frowned slightly in guilt. "That's why we have to find him. Damn, this better not turn out like the catacombs. Once we see that Imogene's okay, I'm going to find the Beekeeper." "

"That's insane," Connor told her.

"It's my best chance of finding Evan," Faye pointed out. "It's better if you don't come with. You're a liability." She pointed to the ax lying on the floor. "Wanna take that?"

Connor refused to touch it. "Just leave it."

This did not bode well for them. Marcus and Betty were less likely to arm themselves with a weapon. Roederer might have, but he was incapacitated. Connor was their best chance of defense. Strike that—not running into the Beekeeper or other homicidal maniacs was their best chance of defense, but Faye doubted that was going to happen.

She snatched up the ax. "You'd better keep it with you."

Connor reached out a shaking hand and grasped the handle.

"Good. If you get the chance to leave the shelter, take it. Even if you get separated from everyone else. Promise?"

"I guess." He had no other choice, and getting everyone to leave had been what he had argued for since a murderer made itself known. Connor drew away from her and traced his steps back to the removable wall.

Chapter 20

Faye tried all of the other auditorium doors while calling for Imogene. All were locked. She tried picking the lock, but the pocket knife from her emergency kit slid uselessly out of any hole she poked it through.

The halls were completely silent.

At least they have food and water, she told herself. Nobody had prepared for any long-term stay in the catacombs, and that had been their undoing. They had not expected the mobs to drive them in so far and then they were trapped.

Faye had agreed to go along with Evan into the shelter with the vague idea of protecting him. If they did run into Sandy Meade, she could use her diplomacy skills—which, at the very least, were better than Evan's—to convince her to let them get out alive. And that was only if Sandy had any interest in diplomacy. She doubted they would run into her anyway because she knew that Sandy would prefer to hide.

She was not so sure about the Beekeeper.

Assuming that Sandy and the Beekeeper linked together in their motives, they must want Evan to be found relatively quickly. The sooner he was found, the sooner everyone else could leave Sandy's space.

The garden seemed to be her most promising guess. If the Beekeeper fit his stereotype, he would go to where the bees were.

Faye grabbed some chalk from the nearest classroom that would open and backtracked to the hall by the auditorium, where she tried to recreate Marcus's map from memory. From the gym was the locker room that opened to the secret door, which brought her here. She ended it with the skinny hallway she had just followed, and left it trailing into nothingness.

To the right of her map was lot of empty space that could contain more hallways with more classrooms or offices or torture chambers or whatever anybody came up with in the planning committee of the world's best high school fallout shelter. After choosing what was likely the best path to take, she stood up and went on with her search.

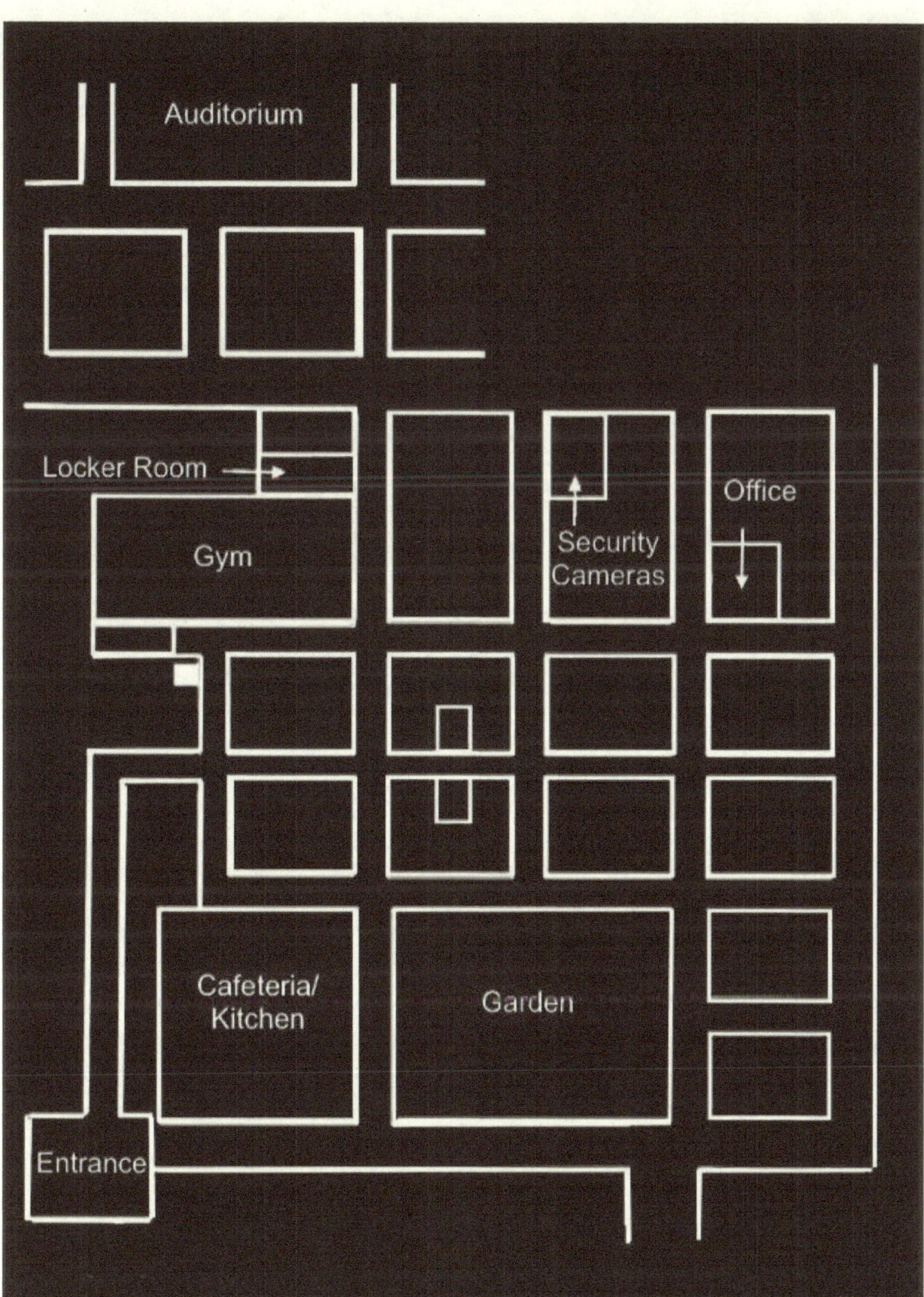
Auditorium
Locker Room
Gym
Security
Cameras
Office
Cafeteria/
Kitchen
Garden
Entrance

Chapter 21

Imogene peeked out the window and caught sight of the two looters talking. Nothing they could say would change her mind that they were looters. Imogene did not buy their story that the war never happened, either. If people still lived on the surface, why on Earth would they come down here when they could travel to other places and see other cities? They could even fly in airplanes.

Imogene would give anything to be able to see other places. She wanted to see the big forests and mountains and fields. She wanted to see the animals so large she could ride on their backs. She wanted to ride in cars and trains and gaze up at tall buildings called skyscrapers. Her father told her about the Sears Tower, the tallest building in the world. At the top, people set up telescopes to look down on the people below them on the sidewalks.

Imogene wanted the looters to be right that there had never been a war and people could live on the surface, but she knew they weren't, or they would not have tried to steal food from their garden. They had food in their own backpacks that Imogene had never seen before, but they could have stolen that from other shelters. It made her mad to see that they were taking a lot more than they needed.

She listened as best she could, but she could not catch what the two teenagers were saying to each other. The girl had an ax that she eventually passed to the boy, Connor's, hand. Imogene could not remember the girl's name. Something short but weird.

The third person with the tan suit was nowhere in sight.

The two looters separated. The girl tracked along all the doors. Imogene heard each entrance shudder as she tried to open it. Imogene crawled on the floor, hiding between the auditorium chairs so the girl could not spot her through the gray-tinted windows. After a long, long time, the girl gave up and walked away.

Imogene stopped just before the center aisle when she saw something moving in the opposite side of the area. She rose to a stand to get a better look.

Not something. Someone. Another girl.

The girl raised her head and glared back at her.

"Are you Sandy?" Imogene asked, louder than she meant to speak. She could not see the girl's face clearly enough to match it with the photo in the yearbook.

The girl crawled toward her.

Betty would say that there were no ghosts, and that this was simply another person, another intruder. Betty was usually right about these things, but Imogene could not convince herself that this girl was a normal human.

She tried to scurry out of the narrow space. She was too slow and too late.

The ghost lunged at her, wrapping her arm around the smaller girl to pin her in place.

Imogene's screaming was cut off as the girl pressed a large cloth in front of her face, blocking her mouth and nose.

Everything in the auditorium went fuzzy.

Chapter 22

Faye opened doors along the way and left them open. Classroom, classroom, empty room, classroom. Chalk dust assailed the air.

She lingered by one classroom door because she thought she heard something breathe.

"Evan?" she asked. She followed along the walls of the room, making sure no shadow went unexplored. She checked the ceiling, looking for a vent or something to explain the sound.

As she pressed her hand against the blackboard, the floor dropped out from under her and she fell.

After landing painlessly, Faye scrambled to her feet. The space was claustrophobically narrow and filthy. Narrow was good: it made it easier for her to climb out. Faye picked up her flashlight, which she had been careful to guard as she hit the bottom of the chute.

She discovered she was not quite alone. A beekeeper suit flopped at her feet. She could not help but feel the body inside the suit as she had gotten up, and she had felt nothing inside but the loose, brittle bones of someone whose body had long since rotted away. She had to wonder who the skeleton once was, and if any missing person report sat open at the police station waiting for closure.

She could gather the suit and the bones to take to the surface, but some old-fashioned idea of not disturbing a grave nestled into her mind. Besides, the living took priority for now.

Faye dug the soles of her boots against the rough cement surface of one wall and planted her hands on the other, then walked upwards a couple of steps at a time. The chute turned out to be longer than she imagined in her fall, because climbing took a long time.

Finally, she grasped the lip of the trap door and tried to pull herself out of the hole. She felt the presence of a body looming over her and smelled the musty scent of old canvas.

Before Faye could raise her head far enough to see the person's face, the figure pried her hands off the floor and shoved her back into the chute.

Chapter 23

Betty sat in silence, trembling. Marcus had pulled out a notepad and was drawing more sketches he could later add to the map. He thought it would be better to reserve the phone battery, as he had no idea how long they would have to remain underground.

Connor had nothing to do except stare at the dummies that littered the floor. It occurred to him that someone might be lying somewhere, pretending to be a dummy while spying on them. Hey, maybe Sandy Meade was lying in the darkened corner and spying on them. He argued with himself that it was not true—Sandy would not be spying on them, because Connor guessed that she would be as susceptible to boredom as any other human being, and she would have attacked them by now.

Leann's breathing whished in and out of her mouth.

Betty had stopped checking on Roederer, so they did have a dead guy among them after all. Shouldn't they do something with the body? What did Betty's pod community do when someone died? If he worked up the nerve to ask, he was sure Betty would answer with some quasi-creepy answer. *We bury them under the gym floorboards* or *we mulch them and sprinkle them in the garden*, while Marcus would note this fact in morbid fascination.

The bell rang.

"It does that every hour," Marcus informed him. "I think they'd be up to fourth period by now."

"You two act like you have all the answers," Betty said. She started rocking back and forth.

"We should just leave." Connor said.

"What about the others?" Marcus asked.

"Imogene's shut up in the auditorium, and Faye's looking for Evan." Connor wondered if he should let them know about Faye but decided against it almost immediately. They would think he had gone insane. "All we have to do is walk down a couple of long hallways, and we'll be back in the modern world with real hospitals and people who know how to handle emergencies."

"We shouldn't leave until we find the others," Marcus said doubtfully.

"This is my home," Betty stated. "I can't leave it."

"Even if it's your only chance of staying alive?" Connor argued a little too zealously.

"It doesn't matter, Betty," a fourth voice echoed from the gym entrance before Mrs. S shuffled out, looking just as crazed as she had in the office shortly before she ran off in panic. "She's not going to let any of us leave."

Chapter 24

Faye ascended the chute a second time, muttering a chain of dirty words for the designer of the trap door. When she reached the top (again), she quickly rolled away from the gap on the floor.

A message had appeared on the chalkboard before her.

I'M WATCHING YOU

"Just hand over Evan, and I'll be out of your hair," Faye answered loudly enough for any spy or listening device to pick up.

No answer of any sort.

She set herself to resume a path of empty classrooms and silence. She opened doors and flooded the hallway with as much light as possible as she went.

Finally, she came across a room that was empty except for a gap in the wall. It slid open silently as she parted the moveable wall to find two blood-ied guards propped on their chairs at an array of dark monitors.

Nobody had mentioned that their eyes had been cut out.

Faye's foot nudged against a frayed strip sticking out from a bouquet of chopped and severed cords. She edged around the puddle of vomit and stepped out into the hall.

After locating the office with the UGLEANN engraved in the door, she picked up her pace as she wound around the hallways. She paid little atten-tion to the route she had followed earlier that day, until a set of sharp metal spikes snapped onto her leg.

Freaking sadists had placed a bear trap in the hall.

Faye ground her jaw in irritation. Though it could not hurt her, it could stall her as she wasted more seconds removing it. Those seconds were piling up.

She bent down and squeezed the springs to pry the trap open. The trap yielded after a few tries. After freeing herself, she closed the trap and posi-tioned it to the side of the hall where it could not catch anyone else.

She proceeded more slowly down the hall. Several more traps lay out, but she kicked them to the side. Most of them were sensitive enough to clamp shut by themselves when they slammed into the walls. Their steel teeth glint-ed brightly under the dim light. Like everything else in the shelter, they bore no obvious signs of aging. Someone must have been tending to them.

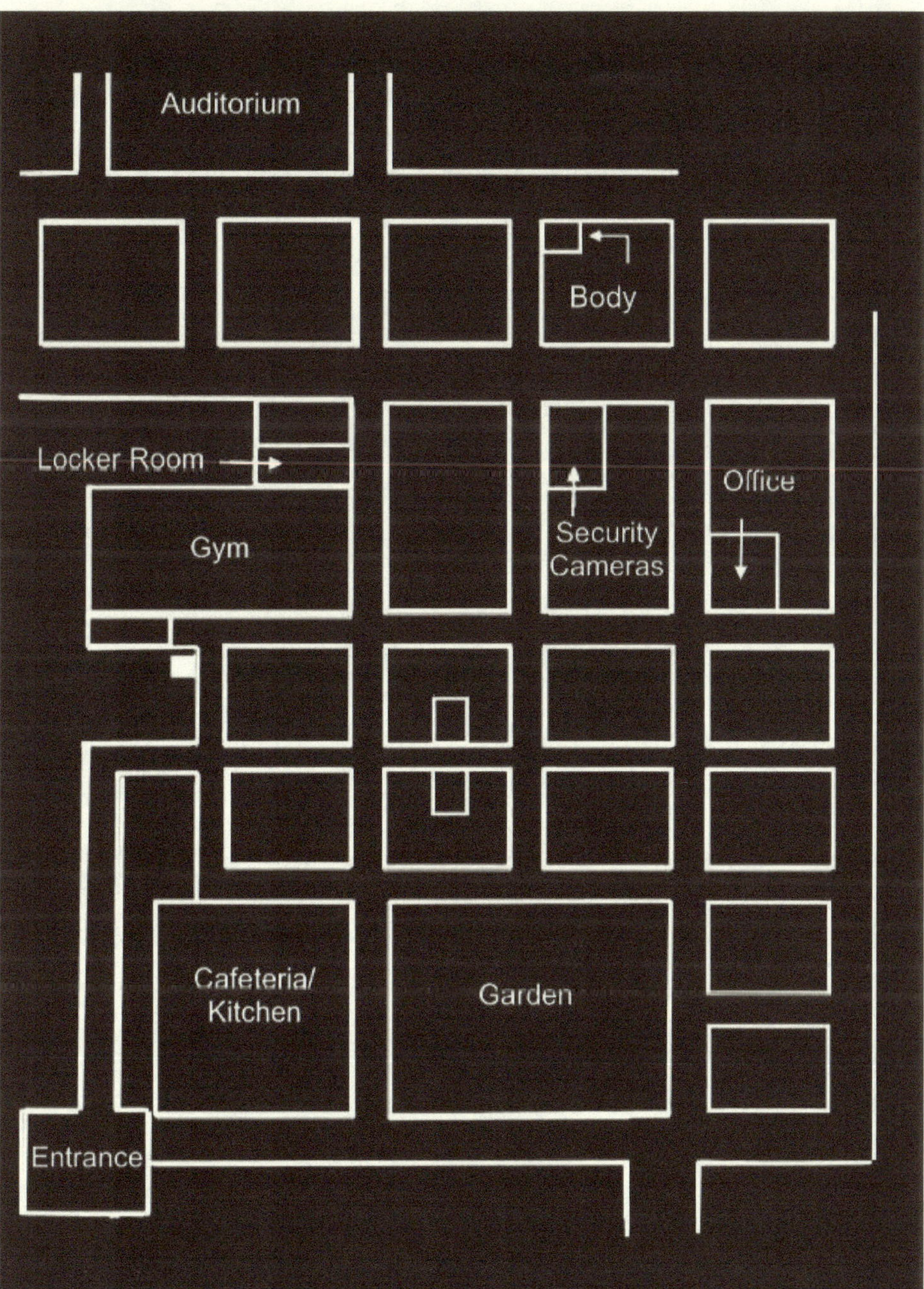
Auditorium
Body
Locker Room
Gym
Office
Security
Cameras
Cafeteria/
Kitchen
Garden
Entrance

Chapter 25

"You told us she was dead," Connor challenged.

"Sandy won't die," Mrs. S proclaimed. She looked at Betty curiously. "You never realized she was there, did you? We were instructed not to talk about her, but that didn't make her disappear. Every day, food went missing from our pantry. And you might have lost a few possessions over the years. Barrettes, pencils, maybe a dress. She took them."

"Why?" Betty asked.

"To remind us that she is still around, watching us."

"So what? If we leave, she won't come after us," Connor pressed on with more surety than he believed. "She won't leave the shelter."

"There's nowhere else to go." Mrs. S's voice rose to a higher pitch. "The world is an irradiated wasteland. She's got us right where she wants us."

Chapter 26

The buzzing sound could be heard as Faye turned the corner and approached the garden. She cast a glance in both directions. She was sure another obstacle would stop her from going in. When no phantom beekeeper popped out from the shadows, she cautiously approached the garden.

Faye opened the door.

The walls and counters churned in yellow and black. Compound eyes and crystalline wings glittered among the shiny, yellow thoraxes and crooked, brown legs. The bees zoomed at her once they saw another surface to engulf.

Faye cupped her hands around her eyes and peered through her shielding fingers.

After a minute or so, she spotted him. A gap of a black T-shirt showed under the crawling mass of bees in the center of the room.

Faye lunged at Evan and pulled him through the room and out into the hallway, where he collapsed. She knelt by him and wiped the bees away, revealing red and swollen skin on his face. The stitches on his hand had broken open, and smears of dried blood caked his arm. She checked his pulse on his other arm. She felt something moving under the skin of his wrist, but it did not beat like a regular pulse. It bulged like something trying to break out of the skin.

Faye tried tilting his head and opening his mouth. Bees crawled from his mouth to hers. She had to stop and spit them out with each attempt. She peered into his mouth and saw an endless procession of them crammed down his throat, more than she could hope to clear away.

Evan made no attempt to breathe. She heard nothing but buzzing and felt nothing but the writhing invasion in his body.

She knew it was too late to save him.

Faye rose and watched as the bees layered themselves back over him.

She had wanted to prevent this from happening. She hoped he meant it when he said he knew about the risks, but did mortals ever really understand? They were always so sure they would survive.

"I'm sorry," she said, her voice barely rising over the persistent droning.

Chapter 27

Marcus passed around trail mix for lunch. Betty took a bag reluctantly, foreseeing that she would need the energy to keep looking after Leann.

"Do you want any trail mix, Mrs. Standicliffe?" Marcus asked.

Mrs. S did not answer. She was too lost in her own memories. Memories of being a seventeen-year-old girl at a school dance when the sirens blared their warning that the world was coming to an end. Running down the stairs to the shelter. Tripping and sliding and skinning her knee as the crowd knocked her down part of the way and scrabbling back up by sheer force of will. Shivering in her torn and mussed dress in the hallways of the shelter while people who knew what they were doing tried to organize the crowd and treat the injured.

In the fifties and sixties, the shelter was set up to protect the best and the brightest students. She was not the best or the brightest. She just happened to be near the exit to the shelter when the sirens sounded.

She had adjusted and carried on with the only life she had available to her. Everything was fine until these unreal children descended into the shelter, thinking they would find ghosts. They claimed that her family and friends and all those people who never made it to the shelter were still alive. They grew older, went off to college, got married and had kids, and traveled around the world. She had no place in that kind of world, where the dead walked around thinking they were alive.

"I still don't understand. Why does Sandy Meade want to kill us?" Betty asked.

"She hates us." Mrs. S hugged her knees, and her fingers dug into her bare calves. "She wants revenge."

"For what?"

"For calling her Sandy Peed. For ripping up her homework. For cutting a hole in her gym shorts. For telling her that she could sit with us at lunch if she crawled around on the gravel and oinked like a pig. For kicking her down in mud puddles. For pinching our noses every time she walked by us. For putting a bee in her sandwich."

"A bee." Connor did not like the mention of bees.

"We stuck it in the peanut butter. When she bit into it, the stinger went into the roof of her mouth, and her face swelled up. They had to call an ambulance."

Betty cringed, growing more repulsed with each admission. "How could you do that?" She aimed a hard gaze at the woman she used to admire.

"I was a different person before the war. A spoiled teenager." Mrs. S pleaded, "Haven't I taught you and the other children to treat each other with respect? Haven't I made you understand how your actions affect everyone in the shelter? I made sure you didn't make the same mistakes I did."

She swiveled her head to look at Connor. "You know Sandy had a huge crush on your father. She was always sneaking around us, waiting for him to notice her."

Connor's mouth felt dry like cotton. "Did he?"

"He tried to be nice. He shouldn't have done that. It only encouraged her to think we would become her friends. We didn't want her around. She was a self-centered girl who liked to play childish games. There were good reasons for that, I suppose, but it was very off-putting to us."

Connor remembered how his father had been furious when he learned about Connor making up that nickname for Leann and getting the rest of the class to use it. *There is no excuse for treating another person like that.* After that, Connor had been forced to write a note apologizing to Leann for teasing her.

"Did you ever apologize to her?" he asked Mrs. S.

"When could I? She was missing and then the bombs . . ."

"You could leave a note," Marcus said. He saw the naiveté in the suggestion as well as the others.

"Why is everyone still here?" A voice from across the gym broke in. It took Connor a moment to recognize Faye. She looked drenched, and she was no longer wearing that fleece jacket. She still had the bag she carried with her, which looked like it had been dragged through dust.

Mrs. S yipped and jumped back, raising her hands out.

"What happened to your clothes?" Betty asked the important question first.

"They got dirty, so I used the shower."

"Did you find Evan? Or Imogene?" Marcus blurted.

"Imogene was still alive the last time I saw her." Faye squatted a fair distance away from them, and Mrs. S scrambled farther away from her.

"Did you see Evan?" Marcus repeated.

A stony look back. "Yeah, I did."

Silence ensued. Connor watched Marcus at first, to see if the other guy would freak out, but Marcus, too, remained silent.

Mrs. S started whimpering. "She killed Imogene. I know it."

"She means Sandy, not you," Connor quickly specified. They did not need any more rifts between them. "She thinks Sandy is taking revenge on us."

"I didn't do anything to her," Marcus said quickly. "Neither did my parents. They lived in Trinidad at the time."

"Doesn't really matter." Connor said. "Evan and Roederer didn't do anything to her either."

"I guess not." Marcus paused before opening his mouth again to muse, "It's too bad Leann isn't awake so she could tell us what she saw. We still don't know why she ran in here."

"Let's worry about that after we get out of the shelter," Faye said grimly.

Betty spoke up. "How do we even know there's a world to return to?"

Faye sighed. She forgot. The others would not survive very long in the world above if they had crossed into another universe and it turned out to be as irradiated as Betty had claimed it was.

"We could check," she thought out loud. "It shouldn't hurt you if we open the door long enough to see if our extra stuff is there."

"What about Imogene?" Betty voiced.

"I'll look for her," Faye said.

"Why you?" Mrs. S cried out, startling everyone.

"Because I don't trust any of you not to run off and get yourself killed."

"You ran off," Marcus accused.

"Marcus, you're not helping."

"You're Death," Mrs. S declared, her legs shaking as she rose to a stand. "You and you." She spun to face Connor. "You put that ax in her head! What are you?"

"What's she talking about?" Marcus looked around wildly, not sure who to ask.

Mrs. S picked up the ax. She held it at her side, ready to swing it if anyone came near.

"Mrs. S." Betty automatically stood up. Connor held her back.

Mrs. S inched back toward the door. Once she stepped beyond the door of the gym to the hallway, she took off running with the ax still in her hand.

Faye glanced back at Connor, Marcus, and Betty. "You might as well go without us," she ordered before she took off after Mrs. S.

Chapter 28

Connor looked over at Leann, who still rested peacefully on the wooden platform. "Should we keep her on the board?" he asked Betty.

"Are you serious?" Betty asked. "We can't go without Imogene and Mrs. S."

"Mrs. S made her choice."

"But Imogene. And we need more people so we can take Roederer."

"Betty!" Connor tried to soften his impatient tone. "Roederer's dead. You know that. Nobody can survive third-degree burns over that much of their body. Faye will look for Imogene."

Tears prickled at Betty's eyes.

"I'm sorry, Betty. I really am. You have to face facts, though. Your home is gone. Hopefully, ours is still there."

Marcus cautiously took her hand and took it as a good sign when she did not pull away from him. "It won't be so bad. We have libraries of books. And you can go to community college and get a certificate for nursing or whatever you want to do."

Betty nodded.

Marcus let go of her hand because he had to help Connor lift the platform.

They could hear echoes down the hallway as Mrs. S continued to shriek in hysterics. "I'm sorry, Sandy! I'm sorry! I shouldn't have done all those things!"

They tuned her out as best they could as they moved down the hallways and into the passageway. Eventually, they reached the door.

They set Leann down, and Marcus tried to crank it open. "It's locked," he said in dismay. "Evan had the key."

Connor braced himself for a journey back through the shelter. He had no idea where Evan was, so he would have to find Faye. "You stay here." He dashed back before either Marcus or Betty had a chance to protest.

Chapter 29

Mrs. S ran straight to her office and locked the door behind her.

The office was in disarray. The children had shifted around the furniture. Mrs. S quickly moved them back into place. The handcuffs were missing from the rungs of the two chairs she had used to lock two of those intruders, but she could imagine that such a measure would be useless. These children were different, and Mrs. S did not know if the nuclear aftermath made them that way or if the surface had any normal humans anymore.

She saw one dusty bottle on the desk that contained pale-blue pills. Her heartbeat quickened as she recognized them. In the first year after the bombs fell, the shelter could receive radio broadcasts from the surface that described what was happening in their corner of the world. One of those reports she and the other inhabitants had listened to declared that the county had brought euthanasia pills for hospitals and clinics. The pills had been reserved for patients who had no hope of recovering from their terminal conditions. A couple of months after that, the reports stopped, and all that they could find on the radio was static.

When she became an official faculty member, Mrs. S learned that the shelter had stockpiled euthanasia pills as well for the shelter's terminally ill inhabitants. Because only the medical staff kept records of the supply of these pills, Mrs. S had forgotten about them. She would have only handled them herself if some irrevocable crisis had occurred that posed an imminent threat to the life of everyone inside.

An irrevocable crisis such as this one.

Besides her, only two of the shelter inhabitants were left alive, but for who knew how long. Austin Barrows' son and his friends could just as easily meet with similar fates.

Sandy had made her message very clear. She wouldn't stop until they were all dead.

Chapter 30

Faye found the office locked tightly. She knocked on the UGLEANN carving, though Mrs. S would more likely cower under the desk than let her in. "Mrs. S? The rest of us are leaving the shelter. Are you coming with?" She strained to hear any sound of a reply.

"Mrs. S?" she asked. She would wait a little longer, as she had with Imogene when she passed by the auditorium on her way back to the gym.

She heard Connor's footsteps echo down the hall.

"Connor's here, too. We're going to the entrance. Are you coming with us?" At this point, she waited only to assure Betty that she really did try to coax the administrator out of her office. Seeing Connor approach, she wondered if there was any more of a slight chance Mrs. S would feel safer in their company. Probably not, as she recalled Mrs. S screaming about how she saw the incident with the ax.

Connor reached the door. "Do you have the key?"

"Evan has it."

"You're kidding."

"Why would I be kidding?"

"You found him, and you didn't think to take the key? You know, in case we needed it to get out?"

Faye let go of the doorknob. "No, I didn't. I was preoccupied."

"I realize that," Connor said, with his burst of anger deflated. Evan was one of Faye's best friends. He reminded her, "The rest of us are still in danger."

"You're always in danger," Faye pointed out. "You're constantly on the verge of getting yourselves crushed, mauled, stabbed, or sick. It's not like it's my job to save you. I'm doing the best I can despite the phantom killer and targeted mass bee stings."

To put an end to this argument, Connor volunteered, "Just tell me where the key is, and I'll get it."

Faye paused. "You said you were allergic to bees, right?" She asked as if he might have lied. *Did he or did he not hear the part about the bee stings?*

"Yeah."

"Then I'd better go. He was in the garden." Faye whirled around and headed toward the dark artery of the hallway that led around the area where they had ventured hours ago. "Go back to the entrance."

Chapter 31

Marcus checked the time again. Fifteen minutes had ticked by since Connor left to get the key.

"Is she okay?" he asked Betty, about Leann.

"She seems stable," Betty said mechanically. She saw no sign of infection or fever. Betty did worry, though, that Leann had not woken up yet.

The above world has hospitals, she reminded herself. If she needed to, Leann could get an honest-to-goodness X-ray. Mr. Dennis had taught them that X-rays were radioactive, but the amounts used were small enough that they would not cause damage as long as they were used sparingly. Despite that, someone had broken the facility's X-ray machine shortly after the war—likely it had been some resident enraged by the losses they had all suffered from the bombs.

She saw the door swing open. Betty scooted closer to Marcus. She could not help but imagine the worst scenarios: violent looters or radiation suit-clad doctors. She summoned the courage to peer out from behind her shielding hand and saw a short brunette looking at them.

"Holy crap, I was just about to call the police," the girl exhaled, then frowned as she aimed her flashlight at them. "Where are Evan and Faye?"

Chapter 32

Evan lay in the hallway right where she'd left him, with bees still crawling over him. Faye did not look closely as she plunged her hand into his pockets until she felt the key. After shaking the bees off, she looped the ribbon around her wrist.

The main hall had darkened as she returned. All the lights they had left on in the course of their exploration had been switched off.

"Connor?" she asked, though she hoped he had made it back to the entrance without running into more trouble. She turned her flashlight on and shone it up and down the hall.

Mrs. S's office door gaped open, and Faye approached the small room. She saw that Mrs. S had draped herself over her desk, her hand gripping an empty pill bottle. Faye nudged her fingers onto the other woman's neck but felt no pulse.

The door slammed shut. Faye whirled around, casting her light on the door. She listened for footsteps but did not hear a single sound from the other side of the door.

Rattling the doorknob did no good, and the door was too thick and strong for her to kick through. Faye searched for the ax, but it was nowhere near Mrs. S's body.

"You're still watching?" she asked the walls. She was not about to go hunting for a hidden camera. Even if she did find one, it would not reveal Sandy Meade. Sandy would remain hidden away from the prying eyes of her unwanted guests.

See, Sandy? I'm not looking.

"I'm not here to find you," she promised. "I understand this is your place. The others don't care about that, either. They just want to get out alive. They won't bother you."

The room gave no cue that anyone was even listening, but Faye knew Sandy must have heard her.

"I know you might not care what happens to them, but this is for your sake, too. There are people on the surface who know we're down here. You may have lucked out with Evan, but if the others don't get out safely, people will be coming down here looking for you. Killing them won't fix it. It'll bring more police, and maybe even the armed forces."

No matter what else happened, she would get out. The only alternative Sandy had was to trap Faye somewhere in the shelter, but Faye found it unlikely that Sandy would want the company. If the legend had gotten it right —and that was a big if—Sandy killed people because she wanted to be alone. It did not matter who ventured into her domain, or whether they tried to seek her out or wandered in by misfortune. Dead shelter inhabitants don't tell tales.

"This includes Betty and Imogene." Faye paused before pleading, "I don't want to do this. I really don't. And it doesn't have to happen. I can get them out, and you won't be bothered by us anymore."

The only sound Faye could hear was her own breathing. She wondered if she had guessed right about what Sandy wanted. Because they were all only guesses. They could only assume this was all about wanting solitude or revenge. Mrs. S could list all the mean things she and her friends did back in the day, but none of them had any real insight into who Sandy had become after all the years she had lived down in the shelter.

Faye turned and jumped back when her beam lit on Mrs. S's body, which had shifted position. The older woman was sitting back on her chair, her lifeless eyes staring through Faye.

Beside her stood the Beekeeper.

The Beekeeper had not been in the room when she entered, so there must be a secret way into the office. How comforting to know that they could have been sitting in the office—with barricades and all—the whole time and the killer could reach them anyway.

The Beekeeper surged forward, hoisting Faye over the shoulder and breaking open the door in one swift motion. Faye managed to twist out of the strong, one-handed grasp and ended up sprawling on her back onto the hallway floor. By the time she lifted her head, she had lost her flashlight and was plunged into darkness.

Faye patted around the floor like Velma from *Scooby Doo*, but the Beekeeper revealed where the flashlight was: by switching the light on for a second and shining it on her before switching it back oP.

She sprang to her feet and dodged away. She did not get far before the Beekeeper slammed against her. Until the unseen, rough hands grabbed her by the neck and locked her in a stranglehold so she could not wiggle free. The Beekeeper dragged her down the hall. Faye tried to slip out of the hold, but her squirming did not even slow her captor's pace.

Faye hit the floor in a drop that was just as jarring as the first tackle in the fight. She got to her feet, ready for another battle. She waited, anticipating the rubbery touch to clamp onto her neck again. The attack did not come. She heard no retreating footsteps, either. The Beekeeper may as well have vanished into the darkness once again.

She brushed her hand on the floor. The rough, cold surface seemed to indicate that she was in the unfinished section.

She crawled to the nearest wall and felt a door. A double door that was bolted shut.

The auditorium, she made a tentative guess.

She could hear faint sounds of someone moving around inside.

Chapter 33

Connor was not entirely sure how he had gotten to wherever he was. The mysterious enemy had made use of Mrs. S's handcuffs, locking him to a chair. He seemed unable to budge the chair from the floor. When he had tested his range of movement, he accidentally kicked a human leg, but the other captive had not made a sound. Connor hoped this captive was only unconscious, but he did not hear any breathing.

He had no idea how long he was there before the Beekeeper emerged, lighting the aisle with a flashlight.

The Beekeeper aimed the beam straight at his eyes.

"You tried to convince me you changed, didn't you," said a feminine voice that seemed to bombard him from all directions in his disoriented state. "That you aren't the same boy who ruined my life."

"Leann?" he finally croaked out the question, though he was not entirely sure of the identity of the disguised girl. Leann should have been lying on that pallet by the entrance, but where he had last seen her hardly mattered, as the girl had plenty of time to spirit herself over to this far corner of the shelter. He did not think it was her, though. This girl's voice sounded different.

"You'd prefer the pretty one? The one who smiled and flattered you with her attention? It's what you're used to, right?"

"If you are . . ." Connor rambled. "Are there two of you?"

"I know you'd rather have her. That's all you care about, isn't it? Pretty girls? That's why you followed her in here. Too bad for you. You're with Ugleann now."

"I didn't mean that," Connor pleaded. He had been eight years old. Connor had thought she would just laugh about it and forget it, like he and most other boys in the class would have done. It had somehow escaped him that Leann was not a boy or a close friend of his and would take it to mean that he thought she was ugly.

"I'm sorry," he repeated. "I was wrong to say that."

"I remember. You were sorry for being so inconsiderate, and you didn't think it would hurt my feelings."

She quoted directly what he had written in the apology letter, the one his father made him send to her.

He thought that the prank had been long forgotten. As stupid and shameful as it was, it should not be worth such an elaborate plot like this.

Not just capturing him, but killing Evan and anyone else unlucky enough to turn up along the way.

Leann—this Leann—must have heard about Evan's grand expedition. Connor doubted that Evan, Faye, and Marcus were knowingly involved. They were too annoyed that her disappearance took priority over their plans. As to whether Leann knew about the people that lived in the shelter? Connor was not about to venture there. His head hurt too much thinking of all the trickery and false identities he'd learned about in such a short amount of time.

They had all been led here so Leann could enact her revenge.

Chapter 34

Faye sidled between the rows of chairs in the back of the auditorium. The Beekeeper came into view first, though the suit bore more dark stains than when they'd last encountered each other. She peered past the suit and the single beam of light and glimpsed Connor. To her relief, he was alive, but the sight of a still, blue-faced Imogene beside him sobered her relief some.

The Beekeeper swiveled to face her. "What are you doing here?" she growled. "I locked you in the office with the crazy teacher."

"You dragged me here. And stole my flashlight." Faye eyed Connor. "Who is this?" She asked as she expected a more straightforward answer from him than from a masked phantom who was kidnapping and killing people.

"She's the real Leann."

"Then who were we carrying around all day?"

Connor tried to shrug, but once again the handcuffs constrained him. His shoulders had started to prickle from lack of movement.

"My foster sister," Leann supplied for them. "She had trouble finding a job, so I paid her to pretend to be me."

Connor still had a pained grimace, so Faye took the initiative to ask."Why?"

"He ruined my life. Do you know where that word Ugleann came from?"

"Connor made it up," Faye guessed accurately. She heard a huff. Leann must have wanted a grander reaction. Too bad Faye did not feel like playing along.

"When I was eight," Connor felt compelled to add. "And I apologized."

"Your father made you!"

"So he called you a name. Which was wrong," Faye hastened to add, "but that wouldn't ruin your life."

Se Beekeeper straightened and clasped at the helmet with both hands. The head appeared to elongate in the dim light, until the helmet separated from the rest of the suit and revealed the wearer's face.

The largest facial tumor spread from her upper lip to down below her chin. A goiter on her neck the size of a golf ball appended to it, propping onto her suit collar. Smaller tumors swelled on the right side of her face, and her thinning hair did not do much of an effective job of covering a couple of bumps at her scalp.

Connor could not help but wince. Faye, too, was taken by surprise, though she contained her horror better. She used to see people with goiters, buboes, and smallpox scars go about their regular business, but those signs of illness rarely appeared in the suburban United States.

"You!" Leann raged. "You made this happen!"

"No." Connor shook his head furiously. Even with all the impossible things he had seen today, he could not have caused this disease.

"You made it happen! You called me ugly! Now look at me! You did this!"

"Connor didn't cause this," Faye said.

"Shut up! You shouldn't even be here," Leann hissed. She stepped back and lifted an arm stiffly in front of her. In her hand, she gripped a small handgun.

She turned back to Connor. "It should have been you. Not me. I lost my home and my parents and spent years in hospitals being examined by doctors who shook their heads and said, 'Sorry. We can't fix you.'" Leann paused, her body starting to sag with fatigue. They noticed. She could feel them looking at her with pity, and that was enough to revive her anger.

"Leann," Faye spoke louder, trying to claim all of the other girl's attention. "You're right. You didn't deserve to go through that pain. But it's not Connor's fault. He doesn't have that kind of power. He's just a boring, dumb human."

"Are you trying to save him?" Leann mocked, putting in extra venom as she uttered the last word. "You couldn't even save Evan's life. He got what he deserved. He thought he was above everyone else because he watched a lot of movies. I bet a lot of kids at school would be glad he's dead."

"He helped save your foster sister," Faye returned. "After what happened to her head. Did you do that?" She very much doubted that the foster sister would have volunteered to risk a concussion.

"She's fine. I got the extra blood from the infirmary downstairs." Leann's voice wobbled a bit, showing a break in her steel-hard resolve. "It must have belonged to them. They weren't supposed to be here."

Faye stepped slightly closer to the end of the aisle, small enough that she did not think it would be noticed. Leann, however, had been paying attention. She had warned Faye what would happen if Faye tried any tricks. At least she thought she had. Whether she did or not, Faye should have known better.

Leann would not let her have the chance to make some sneaky, heroic move.

She pointed the gun at Connor and fired.

Chapter 35

Faye lunged forward but got tangled in the row of seats and ended up falling in the aisle. She propped herself up on her elbows so she could see a triangular dart sticking out of Connor's thigh, and she almost laughed in relief.

A tranquilizer gun?

For a split second, it looked like Leann had played a practical joke on them.

Connor smiled weakly at her as he breathed heavily. The breaths turned into heavier, painful hitches until it seemed like he was choking.

Leann smiled smugly, revealing her intent. "Forgot his EpiPen, didn't he?"

She turned and ran for the exit. The auditorium dimmed as she carried the flashlight away with her.

Chapter 36

Faye sank to her knees by Connor. Carefully, she felt along his denim-covered leg for the dart. His leg jerked as she pulled out the dart.

"Sorry," Faye said. She did not think it was bleeding. She stuck the dart in the chair cushion so she wouldn't cause more damage by letting the dart get accidentally stuck in him again. Other than that, she didn't know what to do. Her experiences around people with allergies were relatively scarce, and if they didn't have the necessary medicine on hand . . .

Connor gasped loudly, struggling with every arrhythmic attempt for air.

Faye drew back her arms and tried to think. She was well aware the brief seconds were whittling away. If she did not find some way to save him, he would die.

Like Evan.

Like the family in the catacombs.

She had been only a chambermaid back then, but the well-meaning idiots handed her their *enfant*, thinking she had a better chance of finding a way out without the rest of the family slowing her down.

She made countless circles around the endless maze of tunnels, finding no food or water, and the child's lungs labored from the chilly air.

Twenty-seven days later, she found a way out: the only one of the party to see daylight again.

Chapter 37

Leann tried to escape through the exit by the left wing. Whatever she had planned afterward, wherever she had gone, no one would ever know. Her death was mercifully quick. She had no time to react before the ax blade sliced into her head.

She fell. Her body dropped to the side, a red line of blood running down her split face. The lone flashlight crashed onto the floor by the curtain.

Despite her pitiable state, Leann had forgotten the fundamental rule of the shelter: it did not belong to her. She should not have involved it in her plan for revenge. Besides the practical element—that no one would ever find the body—she must have thought the symbolism made it appropriate.

She was wrong. Intolerably wrong.

Chapter 38

Faye took little notice of the specter of light rising from the stage and approaching closer. She did not react until the light-bearer placed a hand on her shoulder. Faye shifted to the side. Despite an initial protest voicing its caution in her head, she ignored it, because Connor only had a few short minutes left anyway.

She watched the syringe as the barehanded newcomer removed the cap and inserted the needle into Connor's outer thigh.

Connor's eyes were closed. Between the dim lighting and his weakened blood pressure, he might not have noticed that the hands that administered to him were not Faye's.

It was done. He was breathing again. The dose of epinephrine had given him enough time for Faye to get him out of the shelter.

Chapter 39

After she unlatched the handcuffs, Faye glanced up to see Sandy Meade reclaim the flashlight and aim it at them.

"We're even," Sandy said.

She passed the light back into Faye's free hand and disappeared into the darkness.

Acknowledgments

Thank you to my family: my parents Rob and Martha, and my sister Rory, for inspiring and supporting my love for reading and writing.

Thank you to my friend Gwyn Zmolek, for patiently listening to me talk about this book.

Thank you to Lauren Donovan from The Book Foundry, who had provided a necessary second set of eyes to look over my manuscript for any grammar mistakes or inconsistencies that I might have made. Though, as I have the final say in the more stylistic parts of the story, anything that doesn't make sense in it is my doing, not hers.

Thank you to Geneva (Illinois) Public Library District, for fostering an enthusiastic environment for people who love to read.

Thank you to the people on Reddit's subreddit, /r/selfpublish, for their invaluable advice on how to manage many of the practicalities of self publishing.

About the Author

I grew up in Aurora, Illinois. I love horror stories, ghost stories, and urban legends, and have spent much of my free time delving into various lesser known ones.

I chose the title from a story called "The Shadow Government" from the book *Weird Virginia* by Jeff Bahr, Troy Taylor, and Loren Coleman (published in 2007). The story covers a popular rumor about a plan to install a shadow government if a nuclear war or similar disaster should render the current US government nonfunctional. The negative black and white image of shadowy men in 1960s style suits around a conference table implied that they would be ensconced in an underground fallout shelter.

Basically, I applied this same concept to the history of the fictional school in an unassuming town in the Midwest, which would be designed to gather the best and the brightest students in the area. I would later learn that the concept of schools that would have served as fallout shelters in the 1960s was actually a fairly common phenomenon.

I also learned of the near miss incidents that inspired the making of *The Day After* in 1983. Like during the Cuban Missile Crisis, fears reached an intense high when that movie hit the airwaves. Numerous kids (and adults, I would presume) growing up during the eighties had developed the same types of fears that had amassed in the 1960s: the total annihilation of the world. This round, however, didn't lead to another boom of fallout shelter construction: the feeling evoked by *The Day After*, and its British sister movie *Threads,* was that no amount of preparation would be enough to save humans from the disasters that unleashing nuclear weapons would create, though it did seem to achieve its more successful goal in warning the people in power that nuclear weapons would make for a futile end for everyone.

By the 1980s, the shelter would have gone mostly unattended. During this time, Sandy Meade was rumored to have taken residence in the neglected shelter shortly before the bombs would have fallen in the alternate world. Since then, the shelter has turned into a nether realm hostile to anyone who tries to enter. Bad luck for the main characters, and really bad luck for the alternate world where the survivors did have to take shelter from nuclear war.

www.ingramcontent.com/pod-product-compliance
Lightning Source LLC
LaVergne TN
LVHW051016080826
845145LV00009B/2653

* 9 7 8 0 5 7 8 9 8 0 5 2 2 *